HER CHRISTMAS HOMECOMING

LINDSAY HARREL

If you purchased this book without a cover you should be aware that this book is stolen property. It was reported as "unsold and destroyed" to the publisher, and neither the author nor the publisher has received any payment for this "stripped book."

ISBN-13: 978-1-335-62111-5

Her Christmas Homecoming

Copyright © 2025 by Lindsay Harrel

All rights reserved. No part of this book may be used or reproduced in any manner whatsoever without written permission.

Without limiting the author's and publisher's exclusive rights, any unauthorized use of this publication to train generative artificial intelligence (AI) technologies is expressly prohibited.

This is a work of fiction. Names, characters, places and incidents are either the product of the author's imagination or are used fictitiously. Any resemblance to actual persons, living or dead, businesses, companies, events or locales is entirely coincidental.

For questions and comments about the quality of this book, please contact us at CustomerService@Harlequin.com.

® is a trademark of Harlequin Enterprises ULC.

Love Inspired
22 Adelaide St. West, 41st Floor
Toronto, Ontario M5H 4E3, Canada
www.LoveInspired.com

Printed in Lithuania

"I didn't know. About your late wife."

"I kind of figured. Not even you're that cruel."

Georgia winced, and Nate instantly regretted the words. "I didn't mean—"

"No, it's okay." She looked away. "Anyway, I'm sorry."

"Water under the bridge."

"I—"

"I've got a meeting to run. Guess I'll see you around. Unless you're leaving soon?" Because he didn't need her brand of complicated in his life right now.

"I'm not sure when I'm leaving, actually," Georgia said. "But, uh..."

She speared a glance at the table of committee ladies, all of whom had turned in their seats to watch them.

"Mimi asked me to take her spot on the planning committee." Staring at her cup, she ran her thumb along its smooth lid. "But if you think it's too weird for us to work together, I can bow out gracefully."

"Why would it be weird?"

It was definitely weird.

Lindsay Harrel is a lifelong book nerd who lives in Arizona with her husband and kids. She's held a variety of professional jobs over the years and now juggles school volunteering with being an author and editor. When she's not writing or keeping up with her children, Lindsay enjoys making a fool of herself at Zumba, curling up with anything by Jane Austen and savoring sour candy one piece at a time. Connect with her at lindsayharrel.com and on Instagram.

Books by Lindsay Harrel

Love Inspired

Her Christmas Homecoming

Visit the Author Profile page at LoveInspired.com.

I will say of the Lord, He is my refuge
and my fortress: my God; in him will I trust.
—*Psalm* 91:2

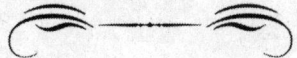

To Dad and Kristin:
Thanks for all the cozy visits, back porch lounging and writing inspiration. I love you both so much and am more than grateful for all you mean to us.

Chapter One

Georgia Carrington had changed a lot since trading the Arizona mountains for the skyscrapers of New York City at the tender age of eighteen.

But from what she could tell, the tiny town of Pineberry had remained frozen in time.

As she drove down Main Street—slowly, in case any elk decided to play chicken with her rental SUV—Georgia breathed through the pangs of loss assailing her.

How had it been thirteen years since she'd come home? She really was a terrible granddaughter.

At least she was here now.

A few stragglers stood outside a smattering of local restaurants despite the forty-degree December first chill in the air. Keeping on Main, Georgia passed the road that led up the hill toward several local farms, then drove on by Pineberry Church—a place she'd been every Sunday from the time she was nine years old, thanks to Mimi. It looked the same as always, with its green-shingled roof, its weathered white clapboard, a light on in the sanctuary for those who needed comfort this Monday evening.

Not Georgia, of course. Not anymore. She was finally more than the drug addict's daughter, and it hadn't been faith that had made that possible. It had taken years of hard work…and years of being away from *here*.

Away from all the distractions of her youth.

Gunning the gas just a tad, she passed the public library. A small portable building, it wasn't much to look at on the outside, but Georgia knew that a cozy fireplace and a pair of armchairs awaited patrons inside. Next came a collection of antique sellers and gift shops, their windows dark given the late dinner hour.

She could see the town hadn't lost the festive holiday touch she remembered from her childhood. Even though Thanksgiving had only been this last Thursday, Christmas wreaths festooned with red and silver ribbons already hung on each of the shop doors, and white lights crisscrossed over Main Street. Against the inky sky, they appeared to be dancing.

The ringtone on her phone split the silence, and her boss's office number showed up on the dashboard screen. With the two-hour time difference, it was nine p.m. in New York City.

Georgia hit the answer button on her steering wheel. "Bob, shouldn't you be home by now?"

"Please." Her boss's gravelly tone filled the vehicle. She could picture him frowning at her, his bushy eyebrows tucked close together as his forehead wrinkled. "You're usually here later than I am."

"But I don't have a spouse and kids waiting for me at home."

"Eh, I had a ton of catch-up to do after the holiday weekend. Maria understands that. And the kids were out late with sports practice and study groups." The rustling of paper filtered from Bob's side of the line. "You've arrived, then?"

"Not quite to my grandma's house, but almost." Her voice hitched at the end. What was wrong with her? She was excited to finally see Mimi, wasn't she? But it had been a long time—too long—since Mimi's last visit to the Big Apple, and Georgia should have come home before now.

She'd just been so busy. At least, that's what she'd told herself. But being here at last, that seemed like a pathetic excuse.

Towering ponderosa pine trees framed the whole street as Georgia wound past the small-town versions of a market, post office, and fire station before turning down Hardscrabble Road.

"Glad to hear it. I hope her recovery goes smoothly. Hip replacement surgery is no laughing matter. My father was down for a few months after his. I'm sure she appreciates you coming out there to help her."

"She actually…doesn't know. It's a surprise. Hopefully a good one." Georgia cleared her throat. "Thanks again for letting me use some of my paid time off on such short notice."

"You're my most dedicated employee." Bob paused. "Speaking of which, I know you need to be there for your grandma, but I'd be derelict in my duty if I didn't remind you of what's at stake back here…and why it would be good if you could return as quickly as possible."

Georgia's tires popped over rocks on the old pavement, and she hit the brights on the SUV so she could see the street signs. Not that she didn't remember which street to turn onto, but having something to do—to read—calmed her nerves. "I know, Bob. The timing is awful." She'd just recently applied for a promotion to financial project director at her staffing and recruiting consultancy firm, and interviews were going to be scheduled any day now.

"My biggest fear is that your absence will give Cathy the opening she needs to schmooze the hiring committee. But I suppose that can't be helped."

Ugh, that Cathy. Always an opportunist. "No, it can't. But do keep me informed, all right?"

"I will."

Mimi's street came within view, and Georgia slowly made the turn. "Thanks, Bob."

After a few more quick office updates, Georgia hung up with a sigh. She couldn't do anything about Cathy or her attempts to undermine all the time and effort Georgia had put into securing a promotion back home. All she could do right now was focus on the task at hand.

Operation Surprise Mimi was back under way.

The houses were sporadically spaced down this road—some close together, and then it would be an acre before another house appeared. All of the homes here were modest, two or three bedrooms and mostly owned by retired folks and young families. The larger homes were a little to the north, off Main Street and Anasazi Way. That's where most of the out-of-town tourists bought their cabins—and where the wealthy families of Pineberry lived.

Families like the Griggses.

It was only one of the reasons that all those years ago, Nate's parents had looked down their nose at Georgia, who had moved to town after her single mom had died of a drug overdose. Of course, nurse and deaconess Frances Carrington was well respected in the community, but not so much that her granddaughter would be good enough for the son of the former mayor. That hadn't stopped Nate and Georgia from falling madly in love their junior year of high school. But Georgia had been a fool.

Because love, then and now, only ever served as a distraction. And Georgia was better off without it.

Finally, her grandma's house came within sight. She pulled into the gravel driveway, cut the car engine, and gripped the steering wheel. Took a deep breath. Released the wheel. Surely Mimi would be happy to see her.

Surely.

After climbing from her vehicle, Georgia grabbed her suitcase and shut the trunk as quietly as possible. A breeze rippled through the trees, a reminder that the warm days of a mountain summer were long past. The air smelled crisp and fresh—so different from the city's aroma of burnt street meat and exhaust—and someone had a fire going nearby. Mimi's porch light wasn't on, and none of the windows were lit. Was Mimi already in bed? It was still only seven, but Mimi was recovering from surgery, so it wasn't outside the realm of possibility.

Georgia rolled her suitcase down the short walk, then hauled it up the front steps of Mimi's house before calling up the flashlight on her phone and scanning the porch for the old turtle statue where her grandma had always hidden an extra key.

Georgia had lost her own copy years ago. She swallowed hard against the thought.

Finally, she located the turtle to the right of the wooden porch swing and lifted it. A Pineberry Medical Clinic keychain with a single key lay on the dusty porch floor. Squatting down, she grabbed it, but on the way up, she hit her shoulder against the porch swing and dropped first the turtle, then her phone. The key slipped out of her hand along with the other items onto the wooden porch, the clatter blasting through the distant hooting of an owl.

Well, if Mimi had been asleep, she probably wasn't anymore.

Her phone's flashlight had gone off—hopefully that didn't mean the screen was cracked, or worse—so she lowered to her knees and swept the ground with her hands in the darkness. Where had that key gone? Finally, her fingers closed around it and Georgia lumbered to her feet. She moved slowly toward the door, trying to fit the key into the lock, which was not an easy feat when she couldn't see either one.

A branch snapped and a step creaked—and she felt someone's presence behind her.

"Stop what you're doing right now and turn around slowly with your hands up." The stranger's voice was deep and forceful.

Georgia squeaked and her heart pounded. Ten minutes in town and someone had called the sheriff on her? Nothing said welcome home quite like that.

Turning, her hands in the air as commanded, Georgia opened her mouth to respond, but was met with a bright light in the face. She blinked and moved her hand to shield her eyes. "I'm not an intruder. I'm—"

"Peach?"

Peach? Nobody called her that except… Oh no. This was so much worse than the sheriff.

And not a stranger after all.

Georgia put her hands on her hips. "You can turn that thing off now, Nate."

"Right. Sorry." Her ex-boyfriend flipped off the light, but it didn't stop Georgia from taking in the shadow of his form under the canopy of starlight filtering through the trees. From what she could tell, the skinny boy from her youth had become a well-built man, with strong shoulders and arms.

Not that it mattered—for several reasons. The top of which was that he was married now.

Though he probably couldn't see her, Georgia cocked her head and folded her arms over her chest to show Nate his presence didn't intimidate her. "What are you doing here?"

"I heard a noise and wanted to make sure Frances was okay."

"I think she's sleeping," Georgia said. "But what, did you just happen to be taking a late-night stroll in the Pineberry slums?" And oops, her tone maybe was a bit harsh, but all the rotten things his parents had said about her family so many years ago just flooded back. How had thirteen years of progress, maturing, and corporate ladder climbing go right out the window just because Nate was here? It was maddening.

"I live next door."

"Oh." And Mimi had never told her? Of course, once she'd heard about his marriage to Stephanie, Georgia had forbidden Mimi from ever speaking about Nate again.

Okay, wow. She needed to get inside and away from this situation pronto before something terrible happened—like Stephanie showing up, slipping her arm around his waist, batting her perfect eyelashes, and asking Georgia how she'd been all these years. Asking whether she had a husband, or kids, as if those were the only accomplishments that were significant.

So yes, she needed to get inside like...yesterday. But even so, Georgia wouldn't let Nate see her sweat. She was used to holding in her emotions back home. It was the only way to survive in a corporate world where everyone looked out for their own interests. Georgia couldn't let the opposition know her weaknesses.

And she couldn't let Nate know them either.

"As nice as this little reunion has been, I should probably go inside." Georgia spun back to the door. "Would you mind pointing that flashlight at the door handle so I can get my key in?"

"No problem." Nate finished making his way up the steps and popped the flashlight back on.

And *of course* he smelled like her favorite flannel candle—a mix of fresh bergamot, soft musk, and heirloom mahogany. Exactly the thing she lit late at night when eating takeout alone in her apartment and reading a novel before bed. Because it was a comfortable smell. A familiar one.

Guess she'd be taking a trip to the store and finding a new candle scent as soon as she returned to New York.

Thanks to the light, Georgia got the key right into the knob and opened the door. Reaching inside, she flicked on the porch light and turned to face Nate. Ooh, possibly that was a mistake, because now she could see him in all his manly glory—his brown hair, slightly longer on top and close-shaven on the sides, a short stubble beard, and blue eyes that popped thanks to the black Henley shirt he wore.

The worst part was that those eyes looked at her, not with disdain—as maybe they should have—but with a mixture of curiosity, pity, and warmth.

None of which was helpful in this moment. She didn't need another reason to be drawn toward Nate Griggs again. Especially now.

But it didn't mean she had to be rude to him either.

Georgia pulled her suitcase inside the doorway and cleared her throat. "Thanks for the help. I—"

"Daddy?" From behind Nate, a girl of about six or seven appeared, and the sight of her punched Georgia in the gut. Because other than her dad's bright eyes, the girl was the spitting image of Stephanie Keyes—the perfect pastor's daughter who had been in school with Nate and Georgia.

The one Nate had married after Georgia had been gone for only six months.

Nate turned. "Honey, what are you doing here?"

The girl's freckled nose scrunched. "Same as you. I wanted to see what that noise was." The girl pointed at

Georgia, her long red ponytail swinging with the movement. "Who's she?"

"It doesn't matter who she is. What matters is that I told you to stay inside. It could have been dangerous—"

"She doesn't look so dangerous to me." The girl turned her big ocean-colored eyes to Georgia and smiled. "Hi, I'm Cassie Griggs."

The gap where her missing front teeth should be was more than endearing, and despite Cassie's parental origins, Georgia couldn't help but smile at her. "Hi, Cassie. I'm Georgia, Frances's granddaughter."

"You're pretty."

The compliment was so sweetly given, with no pretense. Georgia couldn't help but be charmed. "Well, thank you. You're very pretty too." She tapped her temple. "And I'll bet you're smart too."

"Oh, I am. I'm the best reader in first grade and—"

"Cassie," Nate said, moving behind his daughter and pivoting her toward the stairs. "Let's not bother Georgia. Go on home. I'll be right there to tuck you back into bed."

"You always think I'm in the way." Frowning, she turned on her heel and stomped on dead leaves all the way back to the house next door.

Sighing, Nate turned back to Georgia. "Sorry about that."

"It's fine. She's sweet." Georgia leaned against the doorway, arms crossed over her chest. "Didn't want to tell her who I was, though, huh?"

"Well." Nate rubbed a hand along the back of his neck. "It's not that…"

"I get it." She looked at him pointedly. "It really *doesn't* matter who I am."

"Come on, Georgia. I was just surprised to see you after all these years."

She rubbed the tip of her nose. What was she doing, wasting her energy on him like this? Because she *didn't* matter to him. Nate had never really loved her, not if he could move on so quickly.

At first, the loss of him had distracted her. Then, it had driven her. And she would never let him—or any man—distract her like that again.

"It's fine. You should get back to your family now anyway." Georgia faked a smile. "I'm sure your wife will be wondering where you are."

Then, before Nate could say another word, Georgia closed the door in his face.

Keeping several balls in the air at once was not a skill Nate Griggs possessed.

But as he paced the faded beige carpet in his living room, listening to the sound of Cassie's white noise machine coming from her room down the hall and occasionally glancing at the mess of papers on the coffee table, he wished for a crash course in juggling.

He had to figure out what was lacking in his business plan for the youth center. But there was always something more pressing, more urgent. For instance, he'd just gotten a call before his encounter with Georgia—something he couldn't even consider thinking about at the moment—and the news wasn't good. The food truck vendor had to back out of the Christmas festival. That, along with the other setbacks they'd already had, put the festival at serious risk of even happening, much less being the raving success he needed it to be.

Because without the money earned from the festival, there would be no Pineberry Youth Center. And the youth center had been his late wife's dream. He couldn't fail her, not when he'd promised to do everything in his power to make it happen.

Of course, failing people was kind of what he did lately.

He certainly knew he was failing to be the father Cassie needed. One look around the living room was proof of that. Despite the fact that most people around here had their Christmas trees up before Thanksgiving, he hadn't had any time to think of pulling the Christmas decor down from the attic. Besides, decorating together had always been Stephanie and Cassie's thing, and Nate didn't know how to step into the role his wife should have filled without erasing her completely.

A knock sounded on his front door, stopping Nate in his tracks. Who would be here right now? Surely not Georgia... she'd looked at him with such contempt.

"Nate!" The knock came again, along with the familiar voice. Not Georgia, but a man. "Come on, dude. Open up."

"Coming." He hauled open the door and found his cousin on the stoop with a pizza in his hand.

"I come bearing gifts." Christian stomped his boots on the welcome mat. His blond hair hung damp around his shoulders, and his chiseled tan jaw had been recently shaved. "Pizza and an update on the youth center. Plus a Christmas tree strapped to my truck. We can haul it inside later."

"Oh, wow. Thanks. I meant to stop by the construction site earlier, but today got away from me." Stepping aside so Christian could come in, Nate caught a whiff of the pizza. His mouth watered at the smell of the garlic red sauce that Old County Inn—coincidentally, not a place of lodging but a restaurant—was famous for. "And pizza is always appreciated. The PB&Js I made for dinner didn't really stick with me." As if to back up his statement, his stomach growled while he shut the door.

They walked through the tiny living room toward the kitchen, and Christian placed the pizza on the counter while Nate pulled a few plates from the cracked corner cabinet.

"What mayoral duties came up today?" Christian asked.

"Just a minor water dispute, but it took up most of my day."

"Nothing like small-town politics, eh?" His cousin popped the lid on the pizza box, and steam lifted from inside.

"Tell me about it," Nate said, sliding a plate toward him. "Now, what kind of update do you have for me?"

Dad's company might be in charge of construction for the building that would house the youth center, but as the project's foreman, Christian currently knew more about the specifics than Nate did. Ever since Nate had taken office nearly four years ago, he hadn't been involved in the day-to-day details of the family business. Not that he missed it all that much…

"There was a small issue with the siding materials, and that'll delay us a few days. But otherwise, we're right on schedule to be finished by spring so long as the weather isn't a problem."

"That's great." A delay wasn't ideal, especially because snow in December was always a possibility. Still, he knew Christian was doing his best. "Now if I could just get this stupid business plan in order, we'd be golden."

Plopping a huge piece of pizza onto his plate, Christian tsked. "If the brilliant mayor of Pineberry can't figure out the perfect business plan for his pet project, what's the world coming to?" Then he swung over to the fridge and snagged a few glass bottles of root beer.

"Somewhere very dark indeed." Nate grabbed his own slice, shut the box, and walked toward the floral couch he and Stephanie had bought at a garage sale for twenty bucks when they'd been married at nineteen. Such babies who'd had no idea what they were getting into. But they'd had a nice life together anyway—until cancer had taken her eighteen months ago. "And *brilliant* isn't the word I'd use. I'm not sure what exactly isn't right about it, but I have a feeling it won't pass muster at the town council meeting next week."

"Why not? You've been dedicating your life to getting this center up and running for the last year."

"But between all of my other mayoral duties, Cassie, and the Christmas festival—which is another worry itself—I just don't think the proposal is the best it can be." And the five members of the town council, including the incoming mayor, were all shrewd business people with much more experience than himself in that arena.

"Well, I have faith in you, big cousin." Christian lifted his half-eaten pizza slice in salute.

Nate laughed. "I'm only a year older than you."

"And yet you carry a lot more responsibility and weight on your shoulders. But I'm serious. I believe you can do this. You've got more determination in your weird-shaped toe than most people have in their whole body."

"You're the one who broke my toe when we were kids." Nate punched Christian in the shoulder. "You're not allowed to make fun of me for how crooked it is now."

"How was I supposed to know that fishing weight was so heavy?"

Both of them laughed, but then Nate sobered. "Going back to the matter at hand, I don't think determination is going to cut it in this instance. You know I don't really have a head for business and numbers. I'm more of a people person." That's the only reason he'd run for mayor in the first place. Even though his dad had been the one to encourage his son to follow in his footsteps, that was one decision Nate had been fully on board with. He liked helping people, and he'd thought he'd get a chance to do that as mayor.

If he'd known his days would be filled with pushing paper and solving the political problems of a small town—like whether Sally Brightley's house was zoned for a rooster and whether they could reallocate the budgeted money for fixing the park playground equipment toward filling in the potholes on Randall Lane instead—he might have chosen differently. Still, being mayor did give him some discretion over budgetary spending, and that had allowed him to designate the festival profits toward the youth center's first year of operations.

Of course, if Nate didn't get the business plan approved before his term as mayor ended in January, the mayor-elect, Wayne Walker, would try to push his own agenda through. That agenda meant the building would be used instead for a senior adults community center, a choice Wayne favored since it would be more self-sustaining thanks to membership fees—and probably also because seniors could vote for him in the next election.

A senior community center wasn't bad in and of itself. But if Wayne got his way, then Stephanie's dream—to see underprivileged kids in the community have a place to belong—would die.

Christian lowered himself beside Nate and looked at him pointedly. "And yet, when you're done as mayor, you're supposed to take over for Uncle Steve at the construction company. How's that gonna work? Pretty sure you have to do lots of business-y things as CEO."

"That's not what I meant. Dad wants to retire. Of course I'm going to take over for him. It was always the plan."

"I know it was always *his* plan. But what about yours?"

Huffing, Nate sat forward and snagged a bite of pizza, chewing. The pizza was Nate's favorite, with its golden, wood-fired crust and homemade sausage, but even that didn't offer much comfort right now.

Finally, he swallowed. "It'll be fine. It's a good job, and once I'm not mayor anymore, I'll need a job anyway."

"But—"

"I said, it'll be fine."

"You're not the only one who can take over. Not your parents' only child."

Why couldn't his cousin drop it? "You think Eleanor or Aimee want to work construction?" He shook his head, scoffing at the thought. "Ellie's currently overseas and Aims is a lawyer. They've got their own lives."

"And you don't have yours?" Christian pinned him with a look. "I just think—"

"Georgia's back." Nate winced even as the words left his mouth. He'd wanted to change the subject, but couldn't he have selected something better than that? Something less… volatile.

"Reeeeally?" Whistling, Christian set his plate down on the coffee table, crossed his arms over his chest, and sat back against the couch cushions. "What for?"

"She's helping Frances during her recovery."

"Wasn't her surgery like two weeks ago?"

"Yeah."

"So why did she just get here?" His eyebrows lifted, and an amusing sparkle flickered in Christian's eyes. "And how long is she staying?"

Nate sighed, put his plate beside Christian's, and ran a hand through his hair. "I don't know. We didn't exactly have a long conversation."

"But you *did* have a conversation?"

"I thought she was trying to break into Frances's house,

so I kind of ambushed her with a light in the eyes and my deep Terminator voice."

His cousin burst out laughing, and Nate swung a couch pillow at him.

"I'm sorry!" Christian said. "I'm just trying to picture it. I'll bet she got riled about that."

"Maybe a little." Nate couldn't help but grin at the memory of her standing there in the shadows, her pert nose turned sky high as she'd tried her best to make her five-foot-two frame seem intimidating.

Christian rubbed his hands together. "Is she still as pretty as she always was?"

A flame burst to life in Nate's gut. Because while he wanted to deny it, big city looked good on Georgia. Or maybe it was just Georgia that looked good. Either way, in her fancy black New York coat and boots—her blond hair hanging in curls around her shoulders, those cheekbones just as high as they'd always been—the woman was still a knockout.

But that didn't mean Christian had to know that. "She was fine." And was that jealousy pulsing through his veins? Ridiculous.

Christian whistled. "Fine, huh? As in, fiiiiine? Uh-oh."

"I don't mean like that. I mean, she was all right. Okay. Pretty, yeah, I guess, but—"

"Nothing special?"

Nate coughed. "I wouldn't say that." He wasn't a complete liar, after all. "But it doesn't matter anyway. She slammed the door in my face. I think she's still mad at me over the way things ended between us."

"You mean because you refused to move to New York with her when she went away to college? How you insisted on staying home to run your dad's business even though you were madly in love with her, but didn't want to disappoint your parents?"

"Hey. I had responsibilities. I'd made promises. She never understood that. And then she left without a word and excommunicated me from her life."

"I'm not saying she was right to leave the way she did, without really talking things through. Who knows? Maybe she thought you'd come racing after her like they do in those chick flick movies."

Nate side-eyed him.

Christian waved a hand at him. "Or so I've heard. The point is, you were both kids. Now you're not. So…make up."

"It's not that simple."

"Why not?"

"Because." Nate fumbled for an answer. "I'm so busy. And Cassie deserves more of me before I give any time or thought to another woman. And then, there's… Stephanie." Who Georgia seemed to think was still alive, given her parting words to Nate. How did she not know?

"Look, I know you and Cassie have had a rough go of it lately, but she loves you and wants you to be happy. Georgia used to make you happy. And Stephanie…sorry, man, but she's not here. You're not dishonoring her by considering—"

"I'm not *considering* anything." Nate waved away the comment. "I saw Georgia for a split second. She'll be here a few days, then leave." Just like she had before. "Besides, you may remember how happy I was, but all I recall was how miserable I was when she left and never talked to me again."

And it had only served to reinforce what he already knew from childhood—that affections were fickle and often changed when you didn't give people what they wanted.

Even God's love had seemed to grow cold back then. But that made sense. Nate had failed Him too.

"I know her leaving destroyed you, but you came out a stronger man on the other side."

"Thanks." Sighing, Nate gathered up the business plan papers and stacked them neatly together. Maybe he'd work on it tomorrow night. He should probably divert his thoughts to the Christmas festival considering there was a planning meeting in the morning. "Glad you understand this subject is closed."

"What I *understand* is that you're in major trouble, cuz." Grinning, his cousin grabbed his bottle of root beer and took a smug sip. "And it has nothing to do with the fact your business plan needs work…and everything to do with the woman next door."

Chapter Two

The sound of something breaking jolted Georgia awake.

"Fiddlesticks," someone muttered from the kitchen.

Mimi.

Blinking against the light streaming in through the living room curtains, Georgia jumped up from her spot on the couch and rushed toward the kitchen. "Are you all right?"

"Georgia? Is that you?"

She rounded the corner and came face-to-face with her grandma—but not the robust female figure who had gently guided Georgia through the most trying period of her life. Instead, here was Mimi, bent over a walker, her face thinner and more wrinkled than Georgia remembered, her permed gray hair flat on one side. At her feet lay a broken mug.

Georgia picked it up before any of the shards could cut Mimi's bare feet. "Hi, Mimi." Setting the pieces of the mug on the counter, she turned and bit her lip. "Surprise."

"Well, I'll be. This *is* a surprise."

"A good one, I hope."

"Of course, child. Come here." Mimi opened her arms from behind her walker.

It was all Georgia could do not to knock her grandma over with the powerful rush of emotion rolling through her. She gathered Mimi's frail frame to her, and despite the woman's lack of physical strength, it still felt like Georgia was the one being held. "I missed you."

"You too, baby doll." Mimi, who rarely cried, sniffled and pulled away. "Let me look at you. So beautiful, as always. Not enough meat on your bones, though."

"Look who's talking." Georgia swiped at her own cheeks, where a few stray tears had fallen, before pivoting toward the fridge and rummaging until she found a carton of eggs. The rest of the fridge was chock full of disposable containers. "I was going to say that I couldn't wait to fatten you up, but it looks like you don't need me to do much in the way of cooking. You've got enough meals in here to last for months."

"Yes, Elizabeth organized a meal train or whatever they call them these days." Mimi hobbled toward her round oak table and lowered herself into one of the three chairs. "She's even got different church ladies lined up to take me to all of my checkups and other appointments."

Georgia shut the fridge and headed toward the stove, where she found a can of cooking spray and a skillet. "Oh, I thought I might do some of that while I was here." Flipping on the burner, she sprayed the skillet and cracked four eggs into the pan.

"Well, if you'd called, dear..."

"I wanted to surprise you." Georgia combed Mimi's accessories drawer for a wide spatula. There. She reached in and seized it. "But I'm not the only one who didn't call." Spinning, she leaned against the counter and furrowed her brow. "Mimi, why didn't you tell me about your fall? Your surgery? I had to find out from Caroline two weeks after the fact. She said she would have told me sooner, but was out of town when it happened. And then she assumed I knew until she overheard you telling Pastor Jim at church that you hadn't wanted to bother me with it."

"I didn't want you to worry. And I know you're busy."

"You're never a bother to me, Mimi." Georgia rubbed a hand over the pulsing ache in her sternum. "And I'm sorry I ever made you feel like you were."

"I'm just glad you're here now."

"I'm glad too." Blinking fast against a hot flash at the back of her eyelids, Georgia returned to the burner and flipped the eggs. Then she readied two mugs of warm coffee from the pot Mimi must have preset last night. It felt good to serve Mimi for once when her grandma had spent her whole life serving others, but eggs and coffee was hardly a start in repaying Mimi for all she'd done.

Mimi had existed fine without her all these years. Georgia couldn't really expect to swoop in and play the hero after so many years of neglect. The guilt wouldn't be that easy to assuage. But still. She was here now, and she'd do whatever necessary to try to make up for all the times she'd made Mimi feel unappreciated.

With a final flip of the eggs, Georgia plated them quickly and pasted on a fake smile as she made her way to the table and slipped a plate in front of Mimi. "Since you don't need a cook or a chauffeur, let me know if there's anything else I can do to help you while I'm here."

She snagged the mugs of coffee and two forks and slid into the seat across from her grandma, who offered a quick prayer. "Thank you, dear. You know, if you really want to help, I have an idea. But I don't know if you'll be here long enough. Do you know when you're leaving?"

"Trying to get rid of me already, huh?" Georgia smiled as she took a sip of coffee, which was more watered down than she preferred. "I haven't booked a return ticket yet. I'm waiting to hear from my boss about a few things, but for now, I'm on vacation and am happy to do whatever you need. My only plan today was to see you and visit Caroline at her store. Seriously."

Mimi tapped her fork against her plate. "You could take my spot on the Christmas festival planning committee run by the mayor. Obviously, I told him I wouldn't be able to finish out my commitment, but I would feel even better about it if someone with your talents could fulfill my duties."

Georgia's project management background had mostly been used to ensure client's projects stayed on task and under budget, but surely she could apply her organizational skills to a simple small-town event like this. The Christmas festival served as one of her best memories from living in Pineberry. Before that, Georgia had never had a real Christmas holiday that she could remember. Those had left her celebrating on her own, watching old Christmas movie reruns on TV and eating a bag of stale popcorn while her mom slept beside her on the couch—too "sick" to do anything else.

But that changed when Mom died and Mimi took her in.

Sweet Mimi. Georgia owed her so much, and if helping at this festival was one small way to repay her, she was in. "It sounds fun. When's the festival?"

"Two and a half weeks."

"And there's still planning to be done?" Yikes. Or maybe today's meeting was just a formality to remind everyone of their duties. "When is the meeting?"

"In an hour at Pineberry Cuppa. It's a fairly new coffee shop up on Main, right next to the Honey Stand."

"I'd better finish getting ready, then. Are you okay if I stay in the guest room while I'm here? I didn't want to presume, so I slept on the couch last night. I can stay there if you'd prefer."

"It's still your room as far as I'm concerned. I haven't touched anything since you moved out except to keep it dusted and clean." With a pat of her hand on Georgia's, Mimi took a sip of coffee. "You're welcome to stay as long as you like."

Oh, Mimi. "Thank you."

Swallowing against the lump in her throat, Georgia finished her eggs and coffee quickly and took her suitcase to the back bedroom, where boy band posters and quotes from her favorite books still adorned the walls. Then she raced to shower and get ready. She had no idea who she'd see at the coffee shop, but this was her first reappearance in town. No way she wasn't looking her best, just in case she ran into Nate's parents or someone else who had doubted her ability to become someone after her "unfortunate start in life."

After throwing her day-old hair back into a twisted knot, using her straightener to smooth out her side-swept bangs, and putting on a pair of fitted jeans, knee-high boots, and her favorite tunic-style blue sweater, Georgia said goodbye to Mimi and hopped into her rental. She zipped the short distance up Hardscrabble Road and crossed Main into the small lot behind Pineberry Cuppa, an adorable blue building with white shutters that had been a two-story home when Georgia lived here. The breeze nipped at her cheeks as she approached the yellow front door of the coffee shop, which faced Main Street.

Someone else walked up from the sidewalk—and Georgia nearly turned on her heel when she saw who.

Nate Griggs again. Really?

Today he wore jeans and a button-up red flannel shirt over a white T-shirt. A black puffy vest and matching beanie completed the ensemble.

When Nate spotted her, he stopped. Blinked. "Morning." His voice was husky, as if he hadn't spoken much yet today.

And seeing how it was just before 8:30 a.m., that was entirely possible.

"Hi," was all Georgia could manage. She ground her molars. She was intelligent enough—had an MBA from Columbia to prove it—and yet "hi" was all she could say? "Um." Wow. So much better.

She pointed to the coffee shop door, through which she could see the cutest little space with round wooden tables, small vases of flowers as centerpieces, and a chalkboard menu behind a pastry display case. "You going in?"

What was she saying? Of course he was going in.

"I am." He blinked again. "You?"

This was going swimmingly. Georgia pulled her mouth taut. "Yep."

But before she could grab the door handle, Nate pulled it open. The breezy action brought yet another whiff of his delectable cologne under Georgia's nose.

"Thanks." Georgia strode past Nate and walked directly toward the counter to join the short line. Thankfully, Nate—who was greeted with a chorus of hellos—pivoted to the left to chat with some other patrons.

Georgia studied the menu, but the words all swam in front of her eyes. Why had she ever thought she could avoid seeing Nate during this visit? It was impossible. The guy was obviously still entrenched here, and that wasn't changing anytime soon. Georgia just needed to make peace with it and stay as far away from him as possible despite the tiny population and short distance between his house and Mimi's.

The person in front of her finished ordering and it was Georgia's turn. A woman with raven hair and a tiny nose piercing blinked at Georgia from behind the counter. "Georgia Carrington, is that you?"

"Oh, wow. Taylor?"

"Yes, girl. Caroline told me you were back in town for a bit. How are you?" Taylor Dunn tilted her head and zipped her finger up and down. "You look great."

"You're so sweet. So do you." And other than some obviously tired eyes, she did—her tall frame elongated by leggings and a baggy bright green shirt tied at the side. Last she'd heard, Taylor had headed out to Los Angeles to attend school for interior design. They hadn't spoken since Taylor's parents had passed away in a house fire five years ago and Georgia had reached out to offer her sympathies. But Taylor had disappeared off social media after that, and Georgia got busy moving up the corporate ladder. "Do you own this place? It's adorable."

Taylor's smile faltered for a brief moment, but returned just as quickly. "No, just working here part-time until I find something more permanent. I only got back into town a few weeks ago, actually. I'm staying with my brother at the farm for now, but hope to get my own place soon."

"Malcolm owns a farm?" While Taylor's twin had always been outdoorsy, he didn't strike Georgia as the farmer type.

"It's not your typical farm. Remember that old lavender farm up Pineberry Creek Canyon Road?"

"Didn't we go there on a field trip one time?"

Taylor nodded. "The Smythe family used to own it, but when Mr. Smythe died last year, Mrs. Smythe sold it to Mal and moved to Texas to be with her kids. Now he's got goats and llamas up there too. It's a really pretty property, and he's trying to make a go of it."

"That sounds fun."

"You'll have to come visit. Cuddling baby goats is actually better therapy than you'd think." Taylor grabbed a white cup and eyed her. "You look like an Americano kind of girl, am I right?"

"How'd you guess?" Georgia laughed.

"Just the big-city vibe coming off you."

"Is that a good thing or a bad thing?"

"Not good or bad. It's just a thing." Taylor shrugged as she grabbed a Sharpie and wrote Georgia's name and order across the cup. "But speaking of New York, how long until you have to go back?"

"I just got in last night." Georgia checked behind her to be sure their conversation wasn't holding up the line, but nobody was waiting. Back home, there would have been a line of angry customers out the door yelling at her to hurry it up. But here, while about half of the tables inside the shop were full—mostly with older men and women reading newspapers, crocheting, or doing crossword puzzles, but also with a few young moms and their kids—people laughed and smiled, enjoying good food and drinks and the simple activity of being together on this Tuesday morning.

She'd forgotten what a slow pace of life people led up here. The change was kind of refreshing.

Turning back to Taylor, Georgia smiled. "I'm not sure how long I'm staying. A few weeks, maybe?"

"Fun! We definitely need to have a girls' night while you're here. I'd love to catch up more." Taylor capped the marker and set it on the counter. "Oh, and you should come to the Christmas festival if you haven't left yet. Caroline said it's going to be a blast."

"I'm not sure if I'll still be in town for it, but the festival is why I'm here this morning. Mimi asked me to take her place on the committee."

Taylor's eyebrows lifted. "Really?" She leaned in close and lowered her voice. "You know who's in charge of that, right?"

"The mayor. Why?"

Pressing her lips together, Taylor glanced toward the back corner of the shop. Georgia followed her line of sight. A group of four had pushed a few tables together—a group that included Nate Griggs.

He was the only guy in the group, and Mimi had called the mayor a "him."

Georgia's stomach sank. No way. She couldn't be that unfortunate. "Who is the mayor of Pineberry right now, Taylor?"

"I think you know."

Of all the people... "Mimi has some serious explaining to do." Georgia blew out a breath. "In that case, I'm going to need an extra shot of espresso, stat."

Taylor laughed. "You've got it, my friend." When Georgia reached for her wallet, Taylor waved. "On the house this time."

"I'm definitely not in New York anymore."

Taylor shot her a wry grin and started whizzing up her drink, so Georgia casually turned to study the other committee members. She recognized a few—the former librarian, Betty Struss, as well as her third-grade teacher who had to be retired by now and one other white-haired woman who looked vaguely familiar. A few empty chairs sat at the tables. One for her and one for...

A thought struck. Oh no. "Taylor," she said, trying to keep her voice even.

Her friend was just popping a lid onto Georgia's drink. "Hmm?"

"Is Nate's wife by chance on the committee?" *Please say no, please say no.*

Taylor's lips twisted into a frown. "His wife?"

"You know. Stephanie Keyes? Well, Griggs now."

"Girlfriend, I don't know what rock you've been hiding

under." Taylor slid her drink across the counter. "But Stephanie died a year and a half ago from cancer. I thought everyone knew that—even people who've been gone awhile."

"Stephanie passed?" Poor Nate. Poor Cassie. "I had no idea." Her eyes widened. "I was so awful to him."

"Who? Nate?"

"I saw him last night. He caught me breaking into Mimi's house. I couldn't find the key." Georgia placed her hands around the coffee cup, willing the warmth to find its way into her bones. "And I...well, it doesn't matter what I said."

"I take it, given your history, that the reunion didn't go well?"

"That's an understatement." Georgia groaned. "I basically threw his wife in his face...along with the door."

Taylor whistled. "Sounds like maybe you owe him an apology."

Georgia opened her mouth to protest, but Taylor speared her with a look. "I know it totally stank the way he got with Stephanie right after you guys split up. But she was his wife, Georgia. You can't use her against him anymore."

She gripped her drink tight. "Cleary I didn't know she died."

"Does he know that?"

"Guessing so, since I spoke about her in the present tense." Georgia glanced at the ceiling and blew out a breath. "How embarrassing. I...wasn't nice."

"The way I see it, you've got two choices. Be petty, make things extremely awkward, and ruin the time you've got here with your grandma—"

"Really, Tay?" Georgia smirked at her. "That sounds like such a realistic choice."

Her friend laughed. "Or...just say you're sorry, act like adults, and move on."

Sigh. "You're right." Reaching into her wallet, she pulled out a twenty and stuffed it into the tip jar. "That's for the free coffee."

"What about the free and fabulous advice?"

"Remains to be seen how fabulous it is. I'll let you know."

"Don't worry. It'll be okay."

"Thanks for the vote of confidence." Georgia inhaled the warm scent of her coffee. "I think I'm gonna need it."

The moment of truth had nearly arrived. Today Nate would see just how poorly the Christmas festival plans were coming along.

He tapped the table where three of his committee of six—well, five ever since Frances had dropped out—were currently gathered. "I'll be right back, ladies. I'm going to grab us a few refreshments."

Then he headed to the counter, where Georgia was chatting with Taylor Dunn. Despite Nate's best efforts to talk his body out of it, his heart still pounded as he approached. It didn't help that he'd tossed and turned last night after Christian had left. The only sleep he'd gotten had been filled with dreams.

Dreams of Georgia Carrington.

Georgia, who turned at his approach—and looked at him with something different in her eyes. Not disdain this time. Or discomfort.

Well, possibly discomfort, like the kind she'd displayed a few moments ago when they'd met up at the door and she'd barely been able to mumble a hello. He should have felt sorry for her—and sorry for how uncomfortable he clearly made her—but instead, all he could think about was how adorable she was.

Ugh, annoying Christian and his parting words last night.

"I know you always think about what others want, but it wouldn't be the worst thing in the world to occasionally think about what Nate wants." He'd paused. *"Or rather, who Nate wants."*

Nate had shoved his cousin out the door, but the words had made a roost in his brain.

Not that he wanted Georgia. Sure, she was beautiful, but she'd hurt him more than anyone ever had. And he was too busy with this festival and the youth center and Cassie to think about anything else right now, anyway.

Clearing his throat, he nodded at Georgia and glanced over at Taylor, whose eyes trailed between the two of them, her lips pursed together. She probably wouldn't be the only one curious about how the old pair would interact now when they'd once been attached at the hip. Well, Nate would show the town that he could act the professional. Just because there was history between him and Georgia didn't mean they couldn't be entirely civil in their limited interactions.

"What can I get you, Nate?" Taylor asked.

"An assortment of pastries for the group, please. A dozen should do."

With a salute, Taylor grabbed a pair of tongs and began to add muffins, bagels, and croissants to a few different to-go containers.

A soft clearing of a throat made him turn back to Georgia. "Yes?" See? He could be civil.

"I just wanted to say…" She fidgeted with the lid of her white cup, then finally looked up at him with those chocolate eyes he once upon a time would have done anything for.

"What is it?"

"Taylor just told me…well, I didn't know. About Stephanie."

Oh. That. "I kind of figured. Not even you're that cruel."

She winced, and he instantly regretted the words that held more of a barb than he'd intended. "I didn't mean—"

"No, it's okay." She looked away. "Anyway, I'm sorry."

Ah, Georgia. She'd been tough as nails since the day he'd met her when their bikes had collided on the way home from school in sixth grade, but he'd always been able to see the soft center at her core. It was on full display now. "Water under the bridge."

"I—"

"Here you go." Taylor placed the boxes of pastries on the counter. "Oh, sorry. Didn't mean to interrupt. I'll just add it to your tab, Nate."

"No worries. And thanks." He slipped past Georgia, stacked the boxes, and picked them up. "I've got a meeting to run. Guess I'll see you around. Unless you're leaving soon?" His voice hitched up at the end, an unintentional revelation of how much he hoped she'd take off ASAP. Because he didn't need her brand of complicated in his life right now.

"I'm not sure when I'm leaving, actually," Georgia said. "But, uh..."

She speared a glance at the table of committee ladies, all of whom had turned in their seats to watch them. When Nate's eyes met theirs, they pivoted in their chairs again and went back to talking as if they hadn't been spying.

Small towns.

He chuckled and swung his attention back to Georgia. "Go on."

"Mimi actually asked me to take her spot on the planning committee. I didn't know until I got here this morning that you were the mayor. The one leading the committee, that is." Staring at her cup, she ran her thumb along its smooth lid. "If you think it's too weird for us to work together on this, I can bow out gracefully."

"Why would it be weird?" It was definitely weird, but there was no sense in bringing up old junk. So she was going to be on the committee. Big deal.

"Nate." She shot him a look.

He lifted his chin toward the group. "Come on. I've got a whole feast of pastries here. The least you can do after slamming the door in my face last night is take one of them off my hands."

After a moment of hesitation, she nodded. "All right." She indicated he should go on in front of her. "Then lead the way."

They walked toward the group together, and as they took their seats, Caroline Rosche breezed in, mumbling her apologies for being late. She smiled big when she saw Georgia and the two embraced, whispering to each other. Nate took the opportunity to pass around the most recent festival planning document that his secretary, Lois, had compiled.

When Georgia and Caroline took their seats, Nate officially called the meeting to order. "As y'all can see, we've got Frances's granddaughter, Georgia, joining us. Georgia, I'm sure you remember Betty, Susan, and Virginia—or as you'd remember them, Mrs. Struss, Mrs. Landers, and Mrs. Bowers."

Georgia smiled at them all, and they offered her warm smiles.

"It's so good to see you, dear," Betty said. "Your grandma didn't mention you were coming."

"Oh, she didn't know." Was it his imagination, or had Georgia's cheeks pinked up? "It was a surprise."

"It's a wonder you can take a break from your fancy job to be here." Susan worked her crochet needles so fast it was amazing that steam didn't rise from them. "But we're glad to have you."

Caroline placed a hand on Georgia's arm and squeezed.

Smiling, Georgia took the words in stride. "I'm happy to lend whatever help I can to this fun event. Is it like the Christmas festival from when we were kids?" She turned her attention to Nate as she asked the question.

In the background, Taylor ground some beans and for a moment, the whir overtook the soft tones of "White Christmas" playing over the speakers. Nate took the opportunity to pass around the pastries until it was quiet enough to speak again. "Essentially. Although we've had a few changes and setbacks."

"Like what?"

Would Georgia find Nate incompetent when she heard just how many things had gone wrong with the planning? "For starters, our food vendor just canceled. Virginia, would you be able to call around Payson to see if anyone else is available on such short notice?"

"What's that, dear?" Mrs. Bowers cupped a hand to her ear and leaned forward. She must have forgotten her hearing aids at home again. Come to think of it, asking her to use the phone might not be a great idea, as she never could get the hang of the mobile device her kids had purchased for her.

"Never mind, I forgot that I have another job for you." Now he'd just have to think of one. "Is anyone else available to help with this?"

Georgia raised her hand. "I can make some calls if you'd like."

Nate clicked his pen and wrote down Georgia's name next to the item. "Perfect, thanks. Now—"

"Are we really only trying to get one vendor, though?" Georgia plucked a blueberry from the muffin in front of her.

"That was the plan."

"Hmm, okay." She popped the blueberry into her mouth.

He knew that *hmm*. Nate set his pen down. "Did you have a different idea?"

"Maybe. Where is the festival being held?"

"The church."

"Inside or out?"

"Both. Half of the parking lot is going to be undergoing resurfacing, so we had to move the main activity booths inside."

"Would there be space for several food trucks? Say, three or four? It would be nice to give people a little variety."

"The hot chocolate and s'mores truck is always a hit. Why change a good thing?"

Georgia's nose scrunched. "Sounds like you have to change a good thing regardless given that the vendor canceled."

She had a point, but still. "Fine, you can change the kind of food truck, but we've only got space for one, maybe two."

"And you can't rearrange the layout to add more?"

Unbelievable. She'd barely been on this committee for five minutes and she already wanted him to change something as major as the layout. And sure, maybe she had more experience with this kind of thing than he did—he didn't really know, since he had no clue what she actually did for a living—but why not just do the thing he'd asked of her? "I really don't think we need to."

"If it's about the work that rearranging it will take, I'm happy to—"

"Can we move on now?" And man, he hadn't meant to snap. It probably had more to do with his own feelings of incompetence than Georgia marching in here and making him look bad. Not that that was her intention.

He didn't think so, anyway.

Other than the clack of Susan's needles, the other committee members were silent and extremely focused on the treats in front of them. Unnaturally so. Fabulous. More fodder for the small-town gossip mill.

Georgia pursed her lips and shrugged. "Fine."

"Great." Blinking away his frustration, Nate scanned the agenda. Ran a finger under the collar of his shirt. Cleared his throat. "As of the last meeting, we still hadn't found a main stage act to play Christmas music during the festival. Caroline, you were going to work on finding someone for that. How's that going?"

Winding a finger through her shoulder-length brown hair, Caroline frowned. "Honestly, I've been so busy with my store that I haven't been able to devote the time to looking that I should have. I'm so sorry. I'll get right on it."

Tapping her manicured nail against the tabletop, Georgia chewed on her lip. "Don't you think it'll be hard to find someone who is available at this juncture?"

There she went again. Yes, he'd failed miserably so far at making this a go. But did she have to keep pointing it out? He inhaled through his nose, out through his mouth. Slow and steady. "Probably, but what other choice do we have?"

"We could get a DJ?" Susan volunteered.

"Ick, no, Susan," Betty chided. "Remember that year we ended up with the young man whose face was covered in those skull tattoos?" Her features twisted into a grimace. "He scared the children. And me, for that matter."

Nate would chuckle at her horror if the reality of his short timeline wasn't closing in on him. He massaged his temple. "Any other ideas?"

"What if we did a Battle of the Bands?" Georgia asked. "I was involved in a charity event back in New York like that, and it was really successful."

The other ladies murmured for her to continue. All Nate could focus on was her reference to New York. There was pride in her voice, and he felt a prick of something nasty stirring in his gut.

"We could tell them they had to sing family-friendly Christmas songs, and even charge an entrance fee. Local bands would probably jump at the chance to perform. We could hire someone to do lights and sound, build a fabulous stage outside. It could be the main attraction of the festival. Ooh, and I'm not sure what the budget is, but we could rent a few outdoor rides, like a mini Ferris wheel and Tilt-A-Whirl. Really build this thing up so that people come from not just Pineberry and Payson, but even Phoenix. I've got a few contacts in the downtown area that could help us advertise."

Now the ladies were nodding along, their enthusiasm so obvious they looked like those bobblehead dolls that had been so popular when Nate was a kid.

He almost wanted to bobble his own head in response. There was something poised and energetic about Georgia when she was throwing out these ideas. And they were fun ideas, but the scope was going way beyond what this festival was supposed to be. Not to mention the time and effort—and money—that it would take.

Especially if Georgia got the ball rolling and then left to go home.

After all, she didn't know how long she was staying. And if the big city came calling, he had no doubt what she'd choose. She'd proven *that* when she'd left thirteen years ago.

And Nate wasn't going to let her steamroll them all into forgetting her pattern.

Maybe it wasn't fair of him. She was likely only trying to help. But better to not have her assistance at all than to have it and lose it—and be the one left behind to pick up the pieces.

"I'm going to stop you right there." Nate held up his hand. "You seem to have forgotten that this is Pineberry. We don't need some large fancy event. Maybe you've been away too long to remember, but Pineberry is as small-town as it gets. Your big-city ideas won't work here."

Silence descended around them. Caroline gaped at him. Georgia looked at her muffin.

Oof. He'd gone too far. Nate opened his mouth to swiftly apologize, but at that exact moment, in strolled Wayne Walker, the owner of a local bed-and-breakfast—and the next mayor of Pineberry come January.

Grinning, Wayne strode over to their table, tucking his thumbs under his suspender straps. His ten-gallon hat was only half the size of his girth, and that was saying something. "Well, lookie here. How's the festival planning going, Mr. Big Shot?"

Ugh. This guy... "It's going great, Wayne. Now, if you'll excuse—"

"That's not what I heard." Wayne pressed a finger to the side of his nose and studied their little group, chuckling. "That's not what I heard." Then he walked away.

Nate picked up his pen again and gripped it so tight his fingers ached. They just needed to get through this meeting and do the things necessary to make the festival a success.

Because if it wasn't a success, *that man* would win.

And Stephanie's dream would die.

Chapter Three

Mimi obviously didn't need her. So what was she even doing in Pineberry?

Sighing, Georgia set aside the novel she'd snatched off Mimi's bookshelf and stood to pace the living room. She'd spent the rest of Tuesday visiting Caroline at her family's gift shop—the one she ran alone now that her sister had left town for who knew where and her mom had been placed in a local assisted living facility with early-onset dementia—then calling around to pin down a vendor for the festival. Thankfully, it hadn't taken more than a day to find one offering apple cider donuts and hot chocolate who was available on the date in question. She'd also secured the names of a few backups with availability just in case Nate changed his mind about adding more food trucks.

But that was nothing. Not really. She should be doing more.

If only Nate would let her.

Georgia stopped at the fireplace mantel and adjusted the position of Mary and Joseph in Mimi's porcelain manger set. Back home, her own apartment was still bare of Christmas decorations—and probably would stay that way for the whole season for lack of time—but with nothing else to do yesterday, Georgia had dragged all of the Christmas decor out of the attic. Then, with Mimi's direction from her spot on the couch, she'd put up her grandma's six-foot fake tree and covered it with silver beaded ropes, red-drop ornaments, and several papier-mâché balls hand painted by Georgia's mother.

Once she'd allowed the sting of seeing those glance off her heart, Georgia had finished decorating the tree and strung garland along the mantel over the fireplace and gift wrapped wall hangings with paper and big bows to resemble presents.

She'd loved feeling productive, and like there was something she could actually do to help Mimi. But today? She'd exhausted her options. Had spent all day lying around trying to read while Mimi watched old episodes of *Murder, She Wrote*...and felt herself growing more restless by the hour. Someone from church had stopped by to take Mimi to a late lunch and a doctor's appointment in Payson, and the house had been quiet for hours.

Maybe Georgia should take a walk. At the very least, she should get some fresh air. Tossing a jacket on over her sweater, Georgia slipped her phone into her pocket and stepped out onto the back porch, where Mimi had situated a few Adirondack chairs that overlooked the forest behind the house.

She strode to the deck railing, which was out from the porch overhang, and the sun warmed her skin despite the slight bite in the air. Movement from the yard next door caught her eye. There were no fences between yards here— something that her neighbors back home might have been appalled at—so she could clearly see Nate's daughter, Cassie, sitting on a picnic-style wood table on the edge of the Griggses' porch. She was bundled up in a red jacket and matching beanie, and there was a teenager with her. Perhaps a babysitter. School must be out for the day, then.

The teenage girl was arranging some arts and crafts supplies on the table, and Cassie seemed quiet. She picked up a brush, dipped it into some paint, and made strokes across a large piece of paper. Meanwhile, the teenager pulled out her phone at the other end of the table. But it was Cassie who held Georgia's attention. She'd been so bubbly and sweet the other night—up until Nate had told her to leave.

But now, there was something about the way Cassie tilted her head, frowned, and jittered her shoulders as she painted that was familiar. Nate probably wouldn't want Georgia around the girl. But something about her squeezed Georgia's heart.

She was about to head over there when her phone vibrated. One glance at the screen confirmed it was her boss, who she hadn't heard from since three nights ago when she'd first arrived in Pineberry. "Hello?"

"Georgia, glad I caught you," Bob said. "Listen, I don't have much time right now, but wanted to let you know that interviews for the director position are being scheduled for Tuesday, December twenty-third."

"Seriously? The week of Christmas?"

"Yes, yes, I know, but one of the board members on the hiring committee is unavailable before then, and we want this settled before the new year." He paused. "That's not going to be a problem, is it?"

It seemed silly to leave Mimi just before Christmas—part of Georgia had secretly hoped the interviews would be put off until after New Year's so she could celebrate in person with her grandma—but the scheduling was out of her control. "No, of course not. I'll definitely be back by then." It meant she could at least stay for the festival, which was the Saturday night before that.

Not that Nate had seemed like he wanted her help yesterday during the meeting. Clearly, she'd stepped on his toes with her ideas. For the rest of the meeting, she'd been quiet despite the brainstorming that twirled around in her brain. He hadn't wanted to hear it, and she didn't want to butt in where she wasn't wanted.

"Good. And of course, it would be great if you could come back sooner…"

Georgia held in a sigh. "What's Cathy doing now?"

"She's just going out of her way to endear the committee to her. Little things, but I've already caught wind of it turning the tide in her favor." Bob cleared this throat. "I still think your superior work speaks for you, but it wouldn't hurt to come give her some competition."

"I'll think about it." Mimi and Nate didn't seem to need her, after all. She'd accomplished the one task Nate had asked of her regarding the festival.

Perhaps she *should* just go home after this weekend.

"Let me know what you decide. Gotta run."

Bob hung up before Georgia responded, and she blew a breath out through her teeth. Then she glanced over at Cassie again, only to discover her conversation had attracted the girl's attention. The child smiled and waved at her. Her babysitter had disappeared into the house, so Cassie was alone from what Georgia could tell.

How well Georgia knew that feeling.

Slipping her phone back into her pocket, she took the back steps down and cut through Mimi's wild-grass yard toward the table. "Hi, there."

"Hi."

"Mind if I sit?"

Cassie shook her head and slid a bit to the right, making room for Georgia to plop down beside her.

The afternoon sun warmed the table beneath Georgia. Her cheeks too. She pointed to the girl's artwork, where a rainbow of colors—greens, reds, purples, and blues—took up much of the paper. Underneath the rainbow sky stood a red-headed pair...a girl and a woman, holding hands, a forest of trees behind them. "What are you painting?"

"Mommy and me."

Sweet girl. "Cassie, it's beautiful. Did you just start it today?"

"No, I've been working on it after school this week while our neighbor Courtney babysits me. She's inside making me a snack right now. She said I should come inside because it's cold out, but I don't mind being cold. I like being here, where I can see the trees. They make me think of Mommy. She loved the trees." She paused her stream of consciousness and turned her face up to Georgia's. "Do you really think it's beautiful?"

"I really do."

"It's all right, I guess. I think Tommy Delgado would say it's not as good as *his* paintings."

That made Georgia smile. This girl didn't seem to have a filter, and it was delightful. "Well, I don't know Tommy Delgado, and I'm not an expert, but my mom was a painter, so I like to think I recognize talent when I see it. See, she was really good, and she used to tell me all about the techniques she used." Those were some of the most joyful times in Georgia's memory, because whether high or sober, her mother had lit up when talking about art. She'd been happy.

And that had been a rare thing for Brooke Carrington.

"Why'd she stop?"

Ah, that was complicated, wasn't it? "Life got busy." Mostly because of Georgia's appearance when Brooke was sixteen. She'd had dreams—had wanted to go to art school, to become a famous artist—but following Georgia's father to Dallas had prevented that from happening. Then came the death of her spirit when dear old Dad had abandoned them both a few years later.

"Maybe she'll get not-so-busy and start again." Cassie bit her lip and set down her paintbrush. "You could give her my painting, if you wanted. To remind her that she loves it."

Georgia rubbed her chest as if she could massage the pain out of her heart. "That's so sweet, Cassie. But I can't do that."

"It's okay. I can paint another one."

It shouldn't surprise her that Nate's daughter was so generous. He'd always been that way. To a fault, at times.

She wanted to give the girl's shoulders a squeeze, but also didn't want to scare her—after all, they'd just met. Plus, she probably shouldn't even be here. What would Nate say if he saw them talking? He'd clearly been in a hurry to get his daughter away from Georgia on Monday night.

Instead, Georgia patted Cassie on the arm. "My mama's in heaven, just like yours." She really hoped so, anyway. Mama had never talked about her faith, but according to Mimi, she'd accepted Jesus into her heart as a child.

"She died?" Cassie's voice had gone soft.

"Yes. When I was nine."

It took the girl a moment to answer. She just stared at the painting. "I was only five when my mommy died."

"I'm so sorry you had to go through that. That you're still going through that."

"What do you mean, still going through it? It happened at the end of preschool."

"But it's not like you stop being sad just because it's been a while. I'm still sad over my mom's death all these years later." Georgia pointed at the painted figure on the paper. "I used to know your mom. She was very kind and loyal, and I can tell you're a lot like her."

Despite how much it had hurt that Nate married his wife

so soon after he and Georgia broke up, Stephanie Keyes truly *had* been a lovely person. Exactly the kind of girl Nate's parents would have approved of too. "She loved her family and friends very much, so I know she must have loved you and never would have left if she'd had a choice."

Cassie's eyes shimmered with tears. "She told me that she was going to go pick out the best mansion for us in heaven. Do you think she really did?"

"I'm *sure* she really did."

"That's good." Cassie frowned. "I don't think Daddy misses her."

"What makes you say that?"

"I never see him cry. And he doesn't talk about her."

Oh, Nate. "He's probably sad on the inside and doesn't want to make you sad by talking about your mom."

"That wouldn't make me sad." Cassie's voice grew small. "I don't want to forget about her."

"You never will. Not with how much you loved her."

Cassie turned and flung her arms around Georgia's waist, burying her head against her. Georgia immediately returned the hug, soaking up the warmth of this vibrant little girl. Tears stung the backs of her eyes, but why? Why would *this* make her want to cry? Perhaps simply because she felt sorry for the girl.

Just then, the back door of the Griggses' home opened. "Cass—" A pause. "Georgia?"

Georgia turned her head to find Nate on the porch wearing jeans, work boots, a button-up flannel shirt, and a look of confusion. She swallowed hard. Caught in the act. "Hi."

Cassie pulled back from Georgia's embrace. "Daddy!" She hopped from the bench and ran to hug Nate.

"Hi, pumpkin." He pulled back her shoulders gently and studied her. "Is everything okay?"

"It's fine, Daddy. Georgia just came over because she saw me painting." She leaned in closer and lowered her voice—though it was still loud enough for Georgia to hear. "I think because she's bored."

Nate looked at Georgia, eyebrows lifted. "Is she, now?"

Georgia raised her hand. "Guilty as charged."

The corners of Nate's lips twitched.

"Daddy, you're home early. It's usually dark when you get here."

His attention careened back to his daughter. "Yeah, I thought we could get a pizza and have movie night." He tugged down Cassie's beanie, which had popped up a bit. "What do you think of that?"

"I think it would be great! Maybe Georgia can stay too."

"Uh." Nate blinked, then plastered on the fakest smile Georgia had ever seen. "I'm sure Georgia has other things to do."

Thirteen years ago, he would have taken any excuse to hang out with her. And now…this. A breeze kicked up and scraped against her cheeks as Georgia stood. "My grandma will be home soon, and I've got to make dinner. But, Cassie, maybe sometime you could come over and do movie night with me and Mimi if it's okay with your daddy."

Cassie pumped her fist. "Ooh, yes!" Then she pivoted back to Nate. "Would that be okay, Daddy?"

"I'm sure we could work something out."

"Yay!" Cassie did a silly dance. "Oh, is Courtney inside still?"

"Yep, she's still making you a snack."

"'Kay, bye!" And off she raced into the house like an Energizer bunny in red. The sliding door bounced, and Nate moved nearer and closed it all the way. Then he turned back to Georgia and just looked at her.

Suddenly it felt like the temperature had dropped twenty degrees. She slid her hands into her jacket pockets. "You're probably wondering why I'm here."

Nate scratched behind his ear. "Knowing my daughter, she invited you over."

"Not quite, but she did smile and wave." Georgia paused. "She's a really fabulous kid. You've done a great job with her."

"Thanks." His voice sounded so weary, and upon closer inspection, Georgia saw bags under his eyes.

It did things to her heart. Things she didn't want to feel. Because Cassie wasn't the only one Georgia wanted to wrap up in a hug.

Which was ridiculous. Her conversation with Cassie about their mothers had just left her raw. That was all. And Nate was an old comfort.

Old, as in…in the past.

"Well, I've gotta—"

"Do you have any kids?" he asked at the same time.

It was a dart to her heart, but Georgia just shook her head. "Nope. I've got absolutely zero kid experience. Never been married either. I work eighty-hour weeks surrounded by adults who wouldn't mind backstabbing me to get a leg up." Oof. Too much information.

"That sounds…fun. And eighty hours?" Nate whistled. "Doesn't leave much time for a social life."

"Not much, no. But I love what I do." Mostly, anyway.

"And what's that?"

"I started at my company as a corporate project manager out of grad school, and now manage my own team. I've got an interview coming up soon for a director position, though."

Nate blinked at her. "You're a project manager."

"Yes, with an MBA and an emphasis in accounting and finances."

"Oh wow." He scrubbed a hand down his face and laughed. "You really *are* the perfect person to help make this Christmas festival a success, aren't you?"

At least the guy could admit when he was wrong. Georgia raised an eyebrow. "Maybe I am, but I'm not sure I want to be on the committee anymore if you're going to keep biting my head off when you disagree with me."

He groaned. "I'm really sorry about that. There's just a lot of pressure tied to getting the festival right."

"Why? I mean, sure, you're the mayor, but why are you the one running the committee anyway? Don't you have more important things to do?"

"There's nothing more important than the success of this festival." Conviction rang out in his tone.

"I don't understand."

"It's complicated." Nate glanced up at the sky, which had started to darken thanks to the early sunset in December. "Let's just say that if we don't make enough money at the festival, then another project I really care about won't ever see the light of day."

"What project?" She probably should just let it go, but there seemed to be such a sadness to him. Like he had no one to help him carry his burdens.

Not that that was her job either.

And yet...she *could* be here for the festival now. And taking Mimi's spot on the committee was literally the one thing her grandma had asked of her. If she couldn't even do that, how could she make up for neglecting Mimi?

"If you're really interested, I could tell you about it," Nate said, his eyes capturing hers. "Or better yet, I could show you. Do you really have to make dinner right now, or was that an excuse?"

"Mostly an excuse. Mimi's fridge is stocked full of casseroles."

"You know Pineberry." Nate grinned. "So...you *don't* have plans for tonight?"

Georgia folded her arms over her chest. "Not unless you count reading or finding something to binge watch on TV once Mimi goes to bed by eight."

"So you're swamped then."

That finally got a chuckle out of her. "Fine, Mr. Mayor. I'll bite. What do you want to show me?"

Something lit in his eyes. "The future of Pineberry."

What was he doing, taking Georgia to the construction site?

It seemed like every time he managed to talk himself out of spending time with her or confiding in her or depending on her, his heart rebelled against his brain.

Then again, he hadn't known of her background in project management when he'd decided all of that.

The fact was, even though Nate hadn't spent much time talking with God after Stephanie's death, He had still provided him with the exact person qualified to help pull this festival into working order.

And Nate didn't take that lightly.

He pulled his pickup truck to the front of the future youth center construction site, which was surrounded by yellow caution tape. It was just after five, and all the shops along Main had closed. The worksite vehicles had already vacated too, which meant he and Georgia would be alone in there. Probably better, as construction sites could be noisy, and he wanted a chance to show her exactly what he'd envisioned.

To determine if she really *was* the right person to help with the festival and help him see his mission through.

"Here we are."

In the passenger seat, Georgia unbuckled and leaned toward Nate to look out his window at the two-story concrete building. "It's a great location, Nate. Right at the center of town. How'd you get the property?"

It *was* a great location—the library on one side, the blink-and-you'll-miss-it Pineberry Historical Museum on the other. "Remember Mr. Rosenberg, the reclusive millionaire?" At Georgia's nod, he went on. "When he died, his grandkids donated the land to the town a few years ago. They didn't want to pay taxes on a 'dead piece of real estate.'"

She snorted. "Their loss is your gain."

"Exactly."

"So...what is it? I mean, what's it going to be?"

"The plan is to make it into a youth center with all kinds of programs—sports, the arts, cooking classes, skills development, free after-school care—you name it. It'll help underprivileged families and provide a place for the kids of Pineberry and local communities to belong. Give them things to do, and maybe even help them discover talents and abilities they didn't know they had."

"This would have been so great when we were kids."

"Right? Growing up in a small town is magical in some ways, but a lot of kids still get in trouble because of boredom. Especially those without a stable home life or parents who are working themselves to the bone to make ends meet and might not be around or have the money to afford anything extracurricular." He cleared his throat. "Want to go inside?"

"Can we?"

He removed his keys from the ignition and jangled them. "I'm the mayor. I've got keys to all the city-owned buildings."

"But you never let the power go to your head, right?"

"I'm a public servant, Georgia. What do you think?"

She only rolled her eyes in response, but there was a slight lift to the corner of her mouth as they climbed from the truck together. Holding up the tape so Georgia could duck under, he caught the scent of her as she passed—like the jasmine flowers that grew in the shade of his yard in the summertime.

He quickly followed and took in the siding. The fiber cement panels had been only partially installed, but given what Christian had told him the other day about the delay in shipment, that wasn't entirely a surprise.

Georgia pointed to the opening where the front door would eventually go. "Looks like you actually don't need a key to get inside."

"Are you saying I'm not so powerful after all?"

"You said it, not me, Mr. Mayor."

He chuckled as they slipped inside, and Nate popped into the front office to grab a few hardhats off the makeshift desk. He placed one on himself and then emerged to find Georgia in the center of the huge open room, turning and taking it all in. She wasn't exactly dressed for a construction site in her jeans, blazer, green shirt, and white Keds sneakers, but there was something right about having her here.

That was probably just the indelible imprint of her that she'd left on his soul, on this town. Didn't mean she belonged in Pineberry *anymore*.

But still. He needed her. Rather, the festival did. And somehow, he had to convince her of that—despite how poorly he'd treated her at the meeting two days ago.

"It's so impressive," she said.

"Our team has done a great job." Nate met her where she stood and held the hat out to her. "Safety first."

Her nose wrinkled. "Did some sweaty guy wear that today?"

"Probably." Nate settled it on her head before she could wriggle away. "There."

She struck a *Vogue* pose. "Is it my color?"

To be honest, the yellow hat clashed horribly with her green shirt, but even then, she was beautiful. "I think every color is your color."

Aaaaand that was a ridiculous thing to say—even if it was the truth.

Georgia went still and blinked up at him. For a long moment, they both just stared at each other until she tugged her gaze away from his. "So, are you going to show me around or what?"

"Sure." Together they walked the space, and he pointed out where the multipurpose gymnasium, including a full-size basketball court, would go. "And over there'll be the Commons, a game room where kids can play foosball, air hockey and ping pong, with a climbing wall. There'll be a kitchen through that doorway so we can host spaghetti dinners and pancake breakfasts. We also want a specially designated area for teens who don't feel like hanging with their younger siblings." He couldn't help how his voice zipped along, the excitement for the whole project building.

Given her nods, Georgia seemed to be tracking with him. "And what about upstairs?"

"There will be four activity rooms so we can host dance classes, karate, that sort of thing."

"Brilliant. And does the center have enough land for an outdoor area?"

His arms folded behind his back, Nate walked beside her. "Yep, that's the amazing thing about this space. There was enough room for the building plus pickleball courts and a soccer and baseball field out back."

"Sounds like you've thought of everything."

His thoughts drifted to the business plan still sitting on his coffee table, unchanged since he'd last had a chance to look it over Monday evening. "Not everything. But it's coming together."

Georgia fidgeted with the hat, tilting it back and forth until she found a comfortable position. Then she stopped and faced Nate. "So this is a great cause and all, but why are you so passionate about this center? And what does the festival have to do with it?"

How to even begin? But if he really wanted her help, he owed her an explanation. "This was Stephanie's dream first. She was a school counselor and saw firsthand how many kids needed this." He studied Georgia to see if the mention of his late wife bothered her, but her face remained neutral. Then he explained how the festival proceeds would go toward funding the first year of the center's operations, and how Wayne Walker's impending mayoral status might make it impossible.

"Which is why you can't afford for the festival to fail."

"Exactly."

"You say this is Stephanie's dream, but I sense a lot of your own passion in it too. Are you planning to take over as the director? The timing of your mayoral end date seems fortuitous."

"No. I'm planning to take over as CEO of my dad's company when my tenure as mayor is over."

This time, Georgia's face actually did contort into a grimace of sorts. And he understood. Him taking over his dad's company one day was the reason he'd told her no when she'd asked him to move to New York City thirteen years ago.

Was it presumptuous to believe that God had brought her back here to help him with the festival? Maybe.

But maybe it was also a chance for closure.

They were back at the front door, and Georgia slipped the hat off her head, smoothing the flyaway hairs. "You don't seem too enthusiastic about the idea of working for your dad." She handed the hat back to Nate.

He shrugged. "I'm not *not* enthusiastic about it."

"Kind of sounds like it to me."

Georgia had always had a way of cutting straight to the heart of a matter. It was both infuriating and endearing. "I'm just excited to finally fulfill my promise to Stephanie, you know?"

"I get that." She inhaled a deep breath. "And if you'll let me, I can help."

"How?" he asked. She couldn't be saying what he thought she was…

"By taking some of the stuff off of your plate with the festival."

"Wait. You're still willing to help?"

"I am. If you're not holding too tightly to anything, let me use my experience to look over the plan and help make this the best festival I can." She gathered her hair over one shoulder, running her fingers through it. "You might as well let me. Other than the times I'm hanging out with Mimi—who, I'm learning, is a busy lady—I'm bored out of my mind."

"Oh, well, if it will help cure your boredom." Nate smirked. "But what if you have to leave before the festival?" Sure, he wanted her help, but he had to know what he was getting into if he was going to hand over the reins.

"I won't. I just found out my interview isn't scheduled until the week of Christmas."

"And you really want to do this?" He studied her. "This isn't out of some sense of…"

"Of what?"

"Forget it." Spinning, he walked back into the front office and replaced the hardhats in their spot.

When he turned back, Georgia stood in the doorway, arms crossed over her chest—eyes on fire. The way they always got when she was mad or passionate or upset by some injustice. "A sense of what, Nate?"

He sighed, knowing he wouldn't get back to his truck without telling her. "Guilt."

She reared back. "Why would *I* feel guilty?" But the frown on her face told him he'd struck a nerve—maybe a kernel of truth, if not the whole truth. He'd always been able to read her so well.

But that was then. Now…who knew *what* she was thinking? "Like I said, forget it." He paused. "I do appreciate your offer of help. You taking some weight off would be amazing. But this is big, Georgia. I need to know that I can count on you."

Georgia pursed her lips. "Nate, I know things didn't end well between us, and that Pineberry and I have a…complicated history. But if I say I'm going to do something, I do it." She tilted her chin up. "Besides, Mimi doesn't need me to do much, but she did ask this of me. So if you'll let me help… I'd like to. Please."

Nate blew out a breath. Looked away.

He hated to trust this woman again, but what other choice did he have? He was failing on his own, and she had the experience he needed. "All right. You've got yourself a job."

Hopefully he wouldn't regret giving it to her.

Chapter Four

Georgia hadn't set foot inside a church in years.

But she was about to.

Her hands still gripping the steering wheel of her SUV, she stared ahead at Pineberry Church nestled in the pine trees right off Main Street. The sun shone this Friday morning in Pineberry, dappling light through the leaves and onto the roof like a heavenly spotlight. Several large decorated wreaths hung on the church, which was strung with unlit lights. Its parking lot extended out in back, providing the perfect place for the festival.

But the festival wasn't why she was here today.

"The ladies inside won't bite, you know."

Georgia's hands loosened on the steering wheel and she turned in her seat toward Mimi beside her. "Not all of them." Because if anyone would be attending the annual church ladies' Christmas social, it would be Nate's mom, Linda Griggs—who'd always been on the church activities planning committee.

"You didn't have to come, dear." Mimi patted Georgia's knee. Had her hands always been so thin-skinned and frail looking? "I hate to think of you being uncomfortable."

"You really wanted to be here, and I'm glad to take you, especially since there's nothing else you'll let me do for you."

"You don't have to do anything *for* me. I'm just glad you're here."

Ah, Mimi. Georgia placed a hand over her grandma's, which was cold. She forced cheer into her voice. "Well, this social is a good excuse to see the space again so I can plan out which booths and tables will go where for the festival."

"I thought Nate had already decided all of that."

Shrugging, Georgia unbuckled. "When he handed over the reins and plans to me last night, he said I could change anything—within reason. And I've already got lots of very *reasonable* ideas." She winked at Mimi before climbing from the vehicle and circling it to open her grandma's door.

Mimi turned in her seat, guiding her feet out slowly and wincing when her foot hit against the door.

It was so strange seeing her like this. As a nurse, Mimi had always seemed full of energy and spirit. Coping with this version of her grandmother was way tougher than Georgia had imagined. "Hang on." She grabbed Mimi's walker from the trunk and brought it around. "Here."

"Thank you, Georgia." With Georgia's help, Mimi slowly stepped out of the SUV. "You're a dear."

"It's nothing." It truly *was* nothing compared with all that Mimi had done for her.

Birds chirped a lovely chorus as they walked toward the front door. A few more cars pulled up and holiday music drifted outside toward them. While Mimi shuffled, Georgia took a peek at the parking lot. The back half was indeed undergoing some sort of repaving, as Nate had said, but the available space was much smaller than she'd imagined. He'd been right. Not a lot of room out here. People would have to park across the street at the library and walk over as it was…

Okay. This was not ideal. But she'd need to wait to see the inside before making a judgment call.

When they finally entered the lobby—the warmth of the space enveloping them—Georgia glanced around the foyer. The space as a whole was very plain—dark blue carpeting, a few chairs lining the windowed wall, and restrooms along the far end, although a set for a life-size nativity made the space more interesting. Maybe they did live nativities during services or something. Which was neat.

Even so...it wasn't what she'd hoped for.

"What's with the frown?" Mimi asked.

"It's smaller than I remember. I don't know if I just grew or if something changed."

"They added that partition there to divide off the sanctuary from some space at the back so people with restless children could leave." Mimi pointed to a television mounted above them. "They turn that on and broadcast the service so anyone sitting out here can still feel like part of things."

"Oh. Well, that's nice, but it definitely diminishes the church's capacity. I was picturing all of the chairs put away, having one big empty space to work with, but perhaps we could divide the activities up." Hmm, yes, that could work. Georgia's mind raced with the possibilities.

Someone popped their head out the door that went into the sanctuary. A woman, about Mimi's age but with more spring in her step. Mimi's best friend, Elizabeth Eaton. Though they looked nothing alike—Elizabeth wore her stylishly cut hair shoulder-length and silver, regularly got her nails done, and shopped at cute but pricey boutiques while Mimi had never cared about any of that—they'd been sisters at heart for many years after becoming widows at the same time when their firefighting husbands had passed in a forest fire more than thirty years ago, before Georgia was born. Elizabeth had remarried in her fifties to a wealthy man who'd retired in Pineberry looking for peace and quiet, and had found her instead.

"There you are, girls!" Her gold bracelets jangling, she rushed forward and hugged Mimi, then turned her smile on Georgia. "Welcome home, Georgia. We missed you so."

Unexpected tears pricked Georgia's eyes—the second time in as many days. "Missed you too, Aunt Elizabeth." Many a night had been spent at her house whenever Mimi worked the late shift at the clinic. It's how Georgia had first really connected with Nate—he'd lived in the same neighborhood as Elizabeth, and they'd started walking home from school in the same direction every day as teens, his younger sister Aimee in tow. "Thanks for letting me join the social last minute."

"Pshaw." Elizabeth waved a hand through the air. "If you hadn't, I'd have hunted you down. Now, grab some food and something to drink, and settle in. We'll have a speaker in about a half hour. I know it'll bless you."

Maybe Georgia could slip out before the speaker. It would give her a chance to peek around some more. "Is the social in the sanctuary? I'd have thought it would be in the banquet hall out back." A separate building was home to the church's classrooms, banquet hall, and kitchen.

"Oh, yes, the banquet hall is being repainted right now."

First the resurfacing. And then repainting? Sure, old buildings took a lot of upkeep, but she'd hoped to have the extra space for the festival. "When will the painting be done?"

Elizabeth tapped her mouth. "Next week sometime, I believe. But then the new flooring arrives!" She glanced behind them and waved. "Lois, Tina, hi!" Maneuvering around Mimi and Georgia, she rushed to greet the next guests.

"Well, that stinks," Georgia muttered.

"What does?" Mimi asked.

Georgia shook her head. "I was just hoping to make use of both buildings for the festival. It wasn't included in Nate's plans, and now I know why. Makes me wonder why they're holding it here in the first place if so much is under repair."

"It's always been at the church."

"That doesn't mean it always has to be, forever and ever, amen."

Mimi moved toward the sanctuary door. "Where else would you have him hold it? Once the youth center is complete, then there will be a large space for gatherings, but otherwise there's nowhere in town that suffices."

Georgia stopped in the hall. "What about the school?" It was tucked away behind the fire station and Ponderosa Market, right off Hardscrabble Road. "There's a multipurpose room there, and all of those classrooms."

"Winter break will be in session, and they've already scheduled a massive deep clean with a company in Payson."

"They won't consider changing it?"

"Nate already asked." Mimi smiled. "Give the man some credit. I know you're looking at the plans from a professional point of view, but don't forget that he's talented in other areas. Doesn't mean he's incapable."

"I never said he was."

"I know, dear. I know. I just don't want your anger and hurt over the past to overshadow the present and ruin a good thing."

"Mimi, I'm not angry *or* hurt. That would be pointless. I'm not that kid who left here all those years ago. I'm stronger and wiser."

Mimi turned to her, lifted a hand to Georgia's cheek, and patted it. "Just because you say you aren't angry or hurt doesn't mean it's so."

Georgia's mouth opened. Closed.

Her grandma smiled softly. "Come now. Let's go enjoy some free food made by my friends, and you can get a peek at the space where we're holding the festival." She leaned forward on her walker and kissed Georgia on the forehead. "It might just surprise you. Nate just might surprise you, too," she whispered.

"I hate surprises, Mimi."

"I know you do. But think about what amazing things come in surprise packaging." She pointed toward the empty manger. "Like Jesus."

"Jesus?"

"Mm-hmm. A king who everyone assumed would come hurtling from heaven with a sword and powerful might to fight for the throne, but came instead as a helpless baby who would give His life."

Oh. "I guess I never thought of it like that." Georgia took a deep breath. "All right. Lead the way."

The wheels of Mimi's walker squeaked as they bumped from the carpet onto the sanctuary's wooden floor, and Georgia followed her inside, where at least forty or fifty women sat at round tables chatting and eating.

Only it didn't look like the sanctuary. Yes, the small stage with a pulpit was still at the far end, and the stained glass window behind it gleamed and glowed like it always had. But today, the space had been transformed into a winter wonderland of sorts.

Strings of lights crisscrossed the space, from one wall to another, with a dip in the middle that, when lit, created a gorgeous halo effect. Ribbons and large bows adorned the windows, which lined the walls, and there was a pair of Christmas trees flanking the stage. Glass ornaments twinkled under the lights. Several six-foot tables had been pushed together and were covered in silver tablecloths, snowflake patterns woven in the fabric with sparkling thread. The assortment of brunch-y pastries and casseroles—along with the smell of bacon, eggs, and chocolate—made Georgia's mouth water.

Huh. Things had always been so staunch and reserved here before. Or maybe that had been her childhood experiences coloring her memories. And yes, it was small...but maybe this place *would* work for the festival after all.

Mimi nudged her. "There's that smile I know and love."

"I just didn't expect it to look this nice in here."

Mimi's eyes twinkled. "Surprise."

If Nate wasn't needed to light the tree tonight, he'd most likely be planted on his couch—just like he'd been all day yesterday and all day today.

Now that Georgia had taken over the festival planning, he could shift his focus to the business plan he'd been largely ignoring. Hopefully he could bring it up to snuff enough to present at Monday's town council meeting—the last one of the year.

"Ooh, Daddy, look!" Cassie pointed at the forty-five-foot Christmas tree standing in front of city hall adjacent to the post office off Main Street. All around them, townspeople strolled in the crisp evening air, shopping at the various booths set up by local vendors along Rusty Road—where the soft glow of wrought iron streetlamps flickered against the dark Saturday night sky—and waiting for the annual tree lighting ceremony to begin. "It's so pretty, and it's not even lit up yet!"

Nate tugged playfully on her purple scarf. "You're right. It's gorgeous. Lois and her team of volunteers sure did a nice job of decking it out with lights and ornaments. You know how many lights are on it?"

"A billion."

"Close. Eighteen thousand."

Cassie's mouth formed an O. She slipped her gloved hand into his. "Do you think that we could fit that many lights on our tree whenever we decorate ours this year?"

"No, but we could try." He paused. "I'm sorry we haven't had time to do that yet, Cass. Daddy's just been…"

"I know. Busy." Cassie frowned for a moment, but then her face lit up at something she saw behind him. "Georgia! Ms. Frances! Over here!" Letting go of Nate's hand, she raced off into the crowd.

Thankfully, her red coat was easy to keep track of, and she hadn't gone far when Nate caught up with her. She was hugging Georgia and saying something to her. Georgia's blond hair fell forward over her shoulders, and she smiled at Nate's daughter, giving Cassie her full attention. In the same well-cut coat and boots she'd been wearing the night they'd reconnected, along with leggings and a red skirt, Georgia stuck out in the crowd of cowboy hats, jeans, and sweatshirts—a swift reminder that she was all New York now.

Something in Nate's chest shifted. He shouldn't let Cassie get attached to Georgia.

But that was Cassie's nature. She was a people person just like Nate, and kind just like Stephanie had been. She was the best parts of them both.

And as her father, he needed to protect her from getting hurt.

He strode forward. "Cassie, I've told you not to run off in a crowd like that."

Cassie cast her eyes downward. "Sorry, Daddy. But I saw my friends."

"You should listen to your father, Cassie." Georgia squatted in front of her. "But thanks for calling me your friend."

Georgia was backing him up? Nate stood there blinking at her for longer than he should have while Cassie started prattling on about how many lights the "ginormous tree" had and how her mommy had loved Christmas and decorating and watching *The Grinch* and other movies with her during the holidays.

Stephanie had been so good at making the season come alive. She'd baked cookies and made cocoa and hung stockings above the fireplace. She'd even hung one for the baby they never got to meet—the one that had brought them to marriage in the first place.

"Our secret little baby," she'd say every time she'd hung it, stroking the soft red fabric. *"But we never forgot you."*

This year, that stocking still sat tucked away in a box in the attic, just like all the other decorations.

"How are you this evening, Nate?" Frances asked, interrupting his thoughts.

He snapped out of his reverie and stuck his hands into the pockets of his winter coat. "Me? I'm fine. Better now that Georgia's taken some of the load of the festival off my plate."

At the mention of her name, Georgia's eyes snapped toward him for just a moment before refocusing on Cassie, who was recounting to her all the booths she planned to visit tonight. "Of course I want some hot chocolate and maybe a cookie. I'd get ice cream but Daddy says I'd freeze my face off."

Georgia's lips curled in, as if she was holding back a laugh. "Your dad is a very wise man."

"She's right," he butted in, unable to help himself. "I am."

Georgia rolled her eyes but kept looking at Cassie. "What else?"

"Well…" Cassie dragged out the word. "I *really* want to do the letters to the North Pole, but I don't know what I wanna ask for this year. And I don't wanna ask for just anything, you know? I wanna ask for something really special."

Georgia nodded along as if she totally agreed with Cassie. His daughter was a thousand percent engaged. Was his ex-girlfriend sure she didn't have kid experience? The woman was like a Cassie Whisperer. Sure, Cass was a friendly girl in general, but the way she'd connected with Georgia so quickly...

He shook his head. Wait. How had he forgotten so soon that he needed to pull Cassie away from Georgia? Apparently she'd temporarily charmed them both. But he couldn't give her the chance to hurt his daughter.

He walked toward Cassie, placed a hand on her shoulder. "Come on, Cass. Let's let Georgia and Ms. Frances enjoy their evening."

"We *are* enjoying our evening, Nate." Frances leaned on her walker and watched him thoughtfully. The woman seemed to have an uncanny ability to quietly observe and read people. "But if you need to run off and do some mayoral things, we understand."

Cassie pouted at him. "Daddy, I wanted to show Georgia how you light up the tree."

Georgia stood and brushed off the knees of her leggings. "You get to light the tree?"

"And me! I get to be his little helper," Cassie said proudly.

"All we do is push the button," he said. "Mayoral privileges and all."

"And he gets to dress like Santa to do it," Cassie whispered—loudly. She giggled behind her hand.

A car honked somewhere behind them, but nothing could distract him from the absolute glee in Georgia's face, the way her laughter trilled through him. "You're kinda skinny to be Santa, don't you think?"

"That's what I said." Cassie threw her hands in the air.

Her exaggerated expression made Nate laugh. "I don't

know. Santa hefts his sack of toys up and over his shoulder, right?" He snagged Cassie and tossed her across his back. She kicked and squealed, making Frances and Georgia chuckle too. "Seems I've got exactly what it takes to be the big guy."

"Daddy! Put me down." But given his daughter's continued laughter, she was loving this as much as he was.

He adored hearing her laugh. Would give anything to be what she needed. To make her dreams come true. But he was failing in so many ways to be everything she needed. How could he, with Stephanie gone?

But he'd never stop trying.

"What in the world is going on here?"

Ah, a voice he knew well—along with its disapproving tone. He promptly put Cassie back on her feet and turned to find his parents there. "Hi, Mom. Dad."

Linda Griggs patted her coifed black hair and tugged at the collar of her quilted jacket. "Hello, darling." She turned her cheek and Nate leaned in to kiss her. In Nate's opinion, she'd always been way too fancy for Pineberry. Then again, she insisted that even small towns had an upper crust—and she intended to be at the tippy top, always.

Nate shook his dad's outstretched hand. "Dad." The former mayor still had a nice, strong grip, but his dad's tall frame bent slightly and his comb-over tried to cover the effects of aging. He was definitely ready to retire, and somehow, Nate would have to switch into CEO mode soon.

The thought didn't sit well with him.

"Good to see you, son." His dad looked behind Nate, where Cassie had gone back to talking with Georgia. Eyes wide—likely at the sight of his ex-girlfriend talking with his daughter—he glanced at Nate's mom and then cleared his throat, raising his voice. "Come give me some sugar, Princess."

"Grandpa!" Cassie ran to him and he hauled her up, swinging her around like a man thirty years younger. Then she spun to Nate's mom and hugged her. "Grandma!" Mom squeezed her and almost instantly let go, as if Cassie was a fish and she a catch-and-release fisherman.

Licking her lips, Georgia hugged herself and looked between his mom and dad. And for the first time since her reappearance, he saw the insecure teenage girl in her.

"Um, Mom, Dad, you guys remember Georgia."

Mom instantly straightened. Her eyebrows lifted as she took Georgia in. Surely Mom knew she was in town—this was Pineberry, after all—but maybe she didn't know that Nate was in contact with her.

"Hi," Georgia said, stone-still.

"Nice to see you, Linda. Steve." Frances reached out and squeezed Georgia's elbow.

"You as well, Frances," Dad replied. "Glad to see you're up and about."

"Yes, and I shouldn't need my walker much longer. Georgia here came down to help take care of me. Isn't she a dear?"

Mom opened her mouth as if to say something, but Dad slipped his arm around her, and she stayed quiet.

"Well," Georgia said. "We're going to go get some of that fudge Cassie's been telling me about. Have fun at the tree lighting." Then she latched on to Frances's elbow and helped her spin around.

Nate turned to face his parents. Cassie was talking to Dad, and Mom took the opportunity to hiss at him. "You'd better not be thinking of starting things up with that girl again."

If there was one thing Georgia Carrington was no longer, it was a girl. Her time away had given her a confidence, poise—and yeah, the curves too—of a woman. But saying so to his mother would only rock the boat. "Of course not, Mom. She doesn't even live here."

"And if she did? You'd let her back into your life—into your daughter's life—after the way she treated you? Leaving like *you* were the dust on *her* feet instead of the other way around?"

He sighed and scrubbed a hand over his face. No matter how he responded, his mom wouldn't be happy. "Like I said... I'm not thinking about starting anything up with her ever again."

Glancing over his shoulder, he caught Georgia still standing nearby—waylaid by Elizabeth Eaton and facing Nate, but not looking his way.

"So you *aren't* spending time with her? That's not what it looked like just now."

"You know I live next door to Frances. I was just talking with them to be polite. And Georgia's helping me with some festival stuff. But that's all."

"That had *better* be all." Mom patted his cheek, and there was a bit of a sting in the pressure. "I'd hate to see you get hurt again."

Then she spun to Dad and Cassie and declared it was time for some hot chocolate. Both of them cheered, and the three of them took off. Sighing, Nate headed into city hall—a two-story brick building where the mayor's office resided, along with a few other local government positions—and changed into his ancient Santa suit worn by many a mayor before him.

A quick glance in the mirror made him laugh. With no beard or padding—just the suit coat, pants, hat, and boots—he made a poor substitute for Saint Nicholas. But wearing the suit for the tree lighting ceremony was tradition, so off Nate went toward the front steps. He signaled local restaurant owner Jason Anderson that he was ready, and Jason got on the PA system and informed the crowd that the program would begin shortly.

Nate stood off to the side while the high school choir sang a few carols on the steps, joining in along with the crowd. His eyes scanned the group and found Cassie and his parents right up front. But he found himself continuing to search, not certain why…until his eyes landed on Georgia.

Despite the gaiety around her, Georgia just stood there frowning, her hands held in front of her. Who or what had upset her? Surely not his mom and the way she'd been less than friendly? Georgia was stronger than that.

Still, maybe she could use a little extra holiday spirit. Before he knew what he was doing, Nate was walking and settled in beside her. He leaned in close so she could hear him over the music. "Someone looks like her baby reindeer was kicked."

She turned—and their faces were closer than he'd intended. Georgia's eyebrows lifted. "Excuse me?"

Nate took a step back. "You just looked upset."

"And you care…why?"

"Can't have a holiday festival coordinator who isn't in the Christmas spirit."

That brought a small smile to her face. "Maybe my mood has nothing to do with Christmas."

"Maybe it should, though. Look around, Georgia. How can you not be happy right now?"

Moving her lips to the side, she studied him, then nodded. "You're right. The thing that was bothering me is a nonissue. Let the holiday spirit commence."

"Just like that?"

"Just like that."

The song ended and the crowd clapped. Jason, a beefy guy

whose jacket strained against his muscles, came back to the center of the steps while the choir filed off. "Give it up again for our awesome Pineberry School's singers!"

The crowd whooped.

"I've got to go collect my little helper for the lighting," Nate said. "But remember. Santa's always watching to make sure you stay in the Christmas spirit."

Rolling her eyes, she waved him away. "Get out of here."

He turned to grab Cassie, but she was there already smiling up at him as she looked between him and Georgia. "Hey, Cass. You ready?"

"Yeah…" She tilted her head.

"What's wrong, pumpkin?"

"Nothing."

Jason cleared his throat. "Nate, you ready?"

Nate's head popped up and he turned to find the crowd—and Jason—staring at him, amusement on their faces. Jason must have already called him up there and he'd been…distracted. "Coming!" Nate grabbed Cassie's hand. "Let's go, little elf."

"Only if Georgia comes too."

Georgia's brow furrowed. "Oh, sweetie, I—"

Cassie's arms crossed her chest. Great. This was not the time for a tantrum. "I want Georgia to help us." Her bottom lip trembled.

Georgia's face took on a panicked look. "Um…"

"Cassie, let's go." Nate tried to infuse warmth into his firm tone. "Everyone's waiting."

"Please, Daddy? Please, please, please? It's Christmas." She folded her hands under her chin and busted out her best weapon: the puppy dog eyes.

Nate groaned. "We can't make Georgia—"

"I'll go. Hey, come on, sweetie." Georgia grabbed Cassie's

hand and turned to Nate. "I don't know about you, but I'm not strong enough to resist that look."

"I've had years of practice, but even I'm fairly powerless against it."

"Nate?" Jason asked again. "You good?"

"All good!" he called. Then he turned to Georgia. "You sure? People will talk."

She seemed to hesitate for a moment, but with another glance at Cassie, she shrugged. "Let them talk. We know the truth."

Yes, they did. And the truth was, he and Georgia would never be an item again.

But as he stood on the steps with Cassie and Georgia, Cassie holding the big tree lighting button in her palms—the crowd counting down around them—his eyes connected with Georgia's.

And when their fingers brushed as they pushed the button at the same time, sending a spray of lights whisking up the tall tree and igniting the dark sky above them…well, for a moment, he forgot that truth.

All he knew was the same spark that had lit up the tree had lit up his soul.

And he hadn't felt that for a very long time.

Chapter Five

She couldn't wait to get out of here.

Georgia fidgeted in her seat inside Pineberry Church's sanctuary, which had been rearranged back into rows of chairs for the Sunday morning service. The chairs around her were filled with many familiar faces, and some new ones too. Georgia was on an aisle, and Mimi sat beside her. Elizabeth and her husband filled in the spots down the line, along with some of her adult stepchildren.

They were all friendly enough, but a few people—mostly friends of Linda Griggs—had looked at her with haughty eyes, likely remembering the girl she'd been. The stain she'd always carried. And then there was Linda herself, who sat with her husband and Nate toward the front, in the same seats they'd always occupied. A place of importance…one Georgia had never been welcome to join them in.

If she needed any more reminders of the way Linda and the rest of her friends saw Georgia, it had been confirmed last night, when she'd overheard her conversation with Nate: *"You'd better not be thinking of starting things up with that girl again."*

And his reply: *"I was just talking with them to be polite."*

It had seemed like more, especially the way he'd sought her out later because she'd looked upset. And then later, when their fingers had brushed and, for a moment, it had felt like the world had fallen away.

Like old times.

But clearly, this wasn't old times anymore. And that was fine with her. She *did* live in New York, and she was up for a big promotion. And sure, maybe she'd felt a tiny spark of something with Nate, but she'd never let a guy—especially someone who had hurt her so badly before—distract her from what she wanted again.

Not like Mom had. Not like Georgia had, when she'd fallen for—and been fooled by—her former co-worker.

Like she'd told Mimi. She was wiser now—wise enough to look past the miniscule attraction she felt toward Nate and remember what was important.

In front of the church, Pastor Jim Keyes—Stephanie's father—spoke with passion about God's love, how He would seek each lost lamb out because of that great love. Finally, the sermon ended and parishioners stood, stretching and chatting, and the quiet of the sanctuary became filled with lively chatter.

Georgia turned to Mimi. "You ready to head home?"

"I usually like to stay and visit awhile. But I knew you and Nate were meeting up to go over festival details, so I asked Elizabeth to give me a ride home today."

Elizabeth popped her head forward and leaned across Mimi. "And of course I said yes. We are going to go to Bandits for lunch if you want to join us first."

"Oh thanks, but Nate is grabbing us some food and we're meeting at his office."

Elizabeth smiled. "Doesn't that just sound cozy."

Mimi flicked her old friend with a printed church bulletin. "Now, Elizabeth, don't embarrass the poor girl." Then she turned back to Georgia and winked. "But do tell me all the lovely details when you get home, okay?"

Groaning, Georgia stood and gathered up her purse. "You two are impossible." She leaned down and kissed Mimi's cheek. "I'll see you in a bit."

As she slipped outside, she heard her name from behind and turned to find Taylor and Caroline there. "Oh, hey, girls." She gave them quick hugs, then wrapped her arms around her middle. Today the sun had chosen to hide away, and the chill was real. Still, the scent of pine and the cleanness of the air were welcome temporary respites from the New York smog.

Caroline put her hand on her hip. "Don't 'oh, hey, girls' us. You've been back almost a week and we still haven't had our girls' night."

"It's probably because she's too busy with Nate." Eyebrow raised in a tease, Taylor shook her can of ginger ale at Georgia. "Isn't that right?"

"No, that isn't right." She yanked them both away from the church's front steps. "Hush up now. You know how rumors are spread in this town."

Caroline snorted. "Yeah, by joining the mayor and his adorable daughter in lighting the tree in front of everyone."

"That wasn't my idea. It was Cassie's. And have either of you ever tried telling her no? Not as easy as you'd think."

Taylor flashed some side-eye at Caroline, then refocused on Georgia, a knowing look on her face. "I don't think Cassie forced you to look at him all swoony."

"I did not."

"Oh, there was swoon written alllll over your face," Caroline said with a teasing grin. "But now that you're helping him plan the festival—"

"How did you know about that?"

"Pineberry," both of her friends said in unison.

"Of course. I'm really starting to miss New York where I don't even know my neighbor's name." She glanced down at the white smartwatch on her wrist. "And as much as I love the third degree, I've gotta go."

"And where might you be going?" Caroline played innocently with the tips of her long brown braid, but flicked her eyes up to meet Georgia's—a smile playing on her lips. "Mimi was still inside."

"Good*bye*. Love you." Georgia started off toward her car, leaving her friends snickering behind her.

"So, girls' night, yeah?" Taylor called.

Turning, Georgia walked backward and shot her a thumbs-up. "Just tell me when."

"I'll text you." Caroline waved.

Shaking her head at their antics—and the assumptions of the whole town—Georgia climbed into her car and puttered the short distance toward city hall, where Nate sat on the front steps waiting for her.

She pulled the keys from the ignition and climbed out with the briefcase she'd left in her vehicle during the service.

He walked to meet her in his dark jeans, a polo shirt, and a brown bomber jacket holding a white bag, which he wiggled in front of her. "Hungry?"

"Starving, actually."

"Come on in." He pulled his keys from his jacket and led her up the stairs and through the front lobby, his sneakers squeaking on the epoxy-coated flooring. The whole place smelled like citrus with a hint of bleach. Fluorescent panels vibrated with light overhead as they headed toward his office down the first hall. He unlocked the office labeled Mayor and pushed inside. "Welcome to my humble abode."

And at eight by eight feet, humble it was—but there was something so very Nate about it too. He'd shoved a small sofa in back with a coffee table, and all available wall space was lined with bookshelves. His weathered oak desk looked like it had overseen many administrations, but it was neat and clean, with nothing on it but a pad of Post-Its, a computer, a cup of pens, and a picture of him, Cassie, and Stephanie.

On the opposite wall was a window that showcased a view of the woods behind city hall. Rain had begun to fall, plinking against the windowpane. The heater kicked on while Georgia settled herself on the couch and turned slightly to face Nate. "Thanks again for giving me a chance to help with the festival. I've already got so many great ideas for how to make it the best one yet." She held up her hand to stop any protest he might have. "But don't worry, I'm keeping it very *Pineberry*."

"I'm never going to live that down, am I?"

"No, Mr. Mayor, you are not." She smiled.

"But I should be thanking you. I'm grateful you stepped in to help." He set the bag on the coffee table and sat beside her, with a cushion's worth of distance between them. "It's given me a chance to work on the center's business plan, which has to be ready to present by tomorrow night's town council meeting."

"Oh?" Mimi had failed to mention a meeting. "It hasn't been approved yet?"

Nate pulled several foil-wrapped items from the bag, along with a stack of napkins. "It's just a formality, but since I won't be overseeing the center's operations once I'm working for my dad's company, then I want to be sure that I've created a clear path forward for years to come." He held up one of the wrapped food items. "I grabbed us some empanadas from PIEbar. It's a new place, but Cassie and I love it. Do you still like loaded baked potatoes?"

"You remembered that?"

"I remember everything, Georgia." He said it like it was no big deal, but did she imagine the hitch in his voice… like the hitch in her heart at his words? "Anyway, this is a loaded baked potato empanada. If you don't like it, you can have one of the others. I got one that's chicken pot pie and a green chile pork too."

"The potato one is good." She took it from his outstretched hand, swallowing hard against a lump in her throat. It was just an empanada. What was making her so choked up? "Thanks."

"Sure. Gotta have some good fuel for our meeting. I want to hear all of your great ideas." He unwrapped his empanada—a golden, flaky, crescent-shaped pastry—and took a bite. Steam lifted from inside, and when he brought a napkin to his lips, she focused on her own food.

Taking a bite, she was hit with nostalgia. All the flavors blended together—the bite of the green onions, the savory comfort of the bacon, the creamy goodness of the cheese. And the potatoes… "Oh my, that's amazing. I can't remember the last time I had a potato."

Nate, who had been preparing to take another bite, lowered his food. "I'm sorry, what? You? The girl who ordered french fries everywhere we ever went, including Mexican food restaurants?"

"I know, I know. But when I moved to New York, I joined a gym that thought carbs were evil." She made a face. "This is making me remember what I've been missing out on."

Nate was quiet for a few long moments, taking bites of his empanada and swigs from his water bottle. Finally, "Do you like your life now? In New York, I mean."

Oh. She placed what was left of her empanada—embarrassingly little, with how quickly she'd scarfed it down—onto the foil and balanced it on her knee. "I really like my job. I feel challenged there, and love that there's potential for growth. My last job didn't have that. There was only one path to promotion and…"

And *Anthony*.

"And what?"

"Let's just say that I foolishly trusted the wrong person—someone who knew I could beat him out for promotion and succeeded in distracting me from my goals."

"How'd he do that?"

"He got me to let down my guard, then used my misplaced trust in him to access my computer and delete important emails so I didn't get my work done. He made me look incompetent. Then when he got the job, he dumped me." Why was she telling him this? It made her sound so pathetic. Like a victim. "I figured it out after the fact and reported him to my manager, but he didn't believe me."

"Yikes. I'm sorry."

She waved her hand as if swatting away a bug. Because that's what the memory of Anthony was. Pesky. "Thanks, but I didn't give up. I quit that job and found my current one. And now I have an interview on the twenty-third for a director-level position. The thing I've been wanting for years is within my grasp."

"Congrats. I always did admire that about you—your determination. You always went after what you wanted and didn't let anything stand in your way."

His words sank in. He surely hadn't meant them that way, but… "Determination is good. But there's a cost for it sometimes. One I didn't even realize until now."

His gaze penetrated hers. "What do you mean?"

She sighed. "I've neglected Mimi."

His shoulders relaxed. "Oh."

Wait. He didn't think she'd meant the cost of their relationship, had he? Surely he saw that they'd been better off without each other. After all, she'd never have achieved what she did if he'd been tagging along—her relationship with Anthony had proven that relationships only distracted. And he'd never have fallen in love with Stephanie. Cassie wouldn't exist.

So, in the end, everything had worked out.

But she still should explain what she meant…in not so many words. "You were right the other day, when you said I was doing this festival planning thing out of guilt. It's the one thing Mimi asked me to do, and I can't deny her that. She didn't have to take me in when I was nine, and yet, she did. And how did I repay her? By running away. By never coming back. I lacked maturity in that area, but I'm here now, and I'm determined to fix what I broke. If I can. To prove to her—to the whole town—that I've changed."

Nate studied her, the edges softening around his gaze. "You don't have to prove yourself to anyone, Georgia. You've always been good enough."

"Tell that to your mother and her friends. I heard what she said to you last night, Nate."

Nate's face paled. "You heard that? All of it?"

"Yes." She wasn't going to back down from the truth. "Every word."

"Georgia…"

"It's fine, Nate. Nothing that was said was a surprise to me at all." She stared at the rest of her food, her tongue longing for the last bite of her beloved potatoes. Instead, she rolled the empanada up in the foil and placed it on the table.

Out of sight. Out of reach.

Because while potatoes had once been a great love, her new life had no room for them. And that was just how it was.

"Now, let's get to work, shall we? This festival isn't going to plan itself."

* * *

How could one thing be going so right…and others so wrong?

Nate felt the weariness in his bones. The long days of dealing with Pineberry residents and their complaints coupled with the stress of trying to spend time with Cassie in the evenings plus working on the youth center's business plan until midnight for weeks…they'd taken their toll.

Especially given how poorly the town council meeting had gone two nights ago.

Ducking out of the rain that hadn't stopped since Sunday afternoon, Nate reached out and knocked on his in-laws' door. The quaint parsonage sat on the back half of the church's property, a skip and a jump from the church itself.

Jim opened the door. "Nate! Come on in. Your quarterly meeting's over already?"

He stepped inside the tiled entryway, which branched off into a living room, a den, and the kitchen. "Lois's son came back from college a bit earlier than planned to surprise her, so we rushed through it."

"Ah, well, you just missed Cassie and Mary." Jim shut the door and waved Nate to follow him down the hall. "They ran over to the market to get fried chicken for dinner. You're welcome to join us when they return."

"Thanks. And thanks for grabbing Cass from school."

"It's never a problem." He led Nate into the living room, which was small but—like the whole house, and his in-laws' personalities—comfortable and welcoming. Quilts draped the back of the couch and love seat, and an antique buffet sat under the mounted television, filled with pictures of Stephanie. Mary had decked out a Christmas tree in the corner, but otherwise, theirs was a quiet celebration of Christmas. Jim saved all of his passion for the holiday for the pulpit. "We love spending time with her."

Nate lowered himself onto the love seat, while Jim sat in his oversized stuffed rocker. "And she loves spending it with you."

"She's a special little girl, that's for sure. So much like our Stephanie—although much more curious and chatty." He chuckled, but there was a sad droop to his eyes too. "Speaking of Stephanie, how is the youth center coming along?"

"Christian checked in with me today, and we're still on schedule to finish building it."

"But what of the business plan? Wayne Walker was rather nasty about it at the town council meeting on Monday, wasn't he?"

The memory still rankled. "Don't remind me. I still can't believe he called me out like that in front of everyone." Nate leaned forward and held his hands together in between his knees. "Though his concerns were valid. At this point, I don't really have a good plan for sustaining the funding past the first year or two, except future festivals. And by Wayne's own admission, he won't be approving a permanent diversion of funds to the center if it can't be sustained on its own."

"And of course he took the opportunity to not so subtly remind everyone that if he had his way and the building was used as a senior adults center, membership fees would help offset the cost of running it."

"Yeah. He's a natural-born politician. Unlike me." A cuckoo clock in the den chimed six o'clock with the twittering of a parakeet. "I'm just so tired of being pulled back and forth all the time. I took this job to help people, but half the time I don't know if I'm even succeeding. This youth center is the first thing I've done that seems like it'll have a lasting impact on the community. But what if it never happens?"

"You've gotta have faith, son." Jim's chair creaked as he rocked it against the wood floor. "I love seeing Stephanie's dream coming to life, but what is it doing to you? You've seemed inordinately stressed lately."

"I just don't want to fail her."

"Be faithful to the things God has called you to, and you won't fail."

"I'm trying. But sometimes it feels like what He's called me to is too hard."

"Not for Him." Jim paused. "You've told me that after your tenure as mayor is over, you're taking over for your father. But I sense a hesitation in that. As if that's more of his vision than yours. Just like this center was Stephanie's vision."

"It's always been the plan."

"Whose plan? Yours? Your father's? What about God's plan? Have you prayed about what He wants for your life?"

"I've already promised to take over so my dad can retire. God honors people who keep their promises, right?" Especially when he'd failed God in so many ways. He had to do right when he was able.

"You're always doing things for others, and that's admirable, Nate. But while God calls us to be helpers, He also placed certain talents and passions in our hearts, and sometimes that's the answer for the direction we should go. Your dad loves you and wants you to do what makes you come alive." Jim rubbed his stubbled chin. "That's all anyone wants for their kids. So, maybe you should consider what makes *you* happy. If it aligns with what also makes you holy…there's where true joy lies."

"I get what you're saying, Jim. And I appreciate it. But I wouldn't even know where to start in thinking about another option. I can't let my family down. It's why I stayed in Pineberry all those years ago instead of…"

"Instead of following Georgia Carrington to New York?"

Nate stared at him. "You know about that?"

"Of course, son. You were friends with Stephanie before you started dating her. She was worried about you and asked us to pray for you." He smiled, pride shining in his eyes. "I've always loved how God brought the two of you together, despite your broken hearts. You were the perfect mate for her."

Nate coughed, emotion clogging his throat. "The truth is, Stephanie deserved better than me."

He may never have loved Stephanie in the same passionate-lose-all-reason way he'd loved Georgia, but when she'd fallen pregnant, he'd done what he thought was the right thing. Married her. Eventually, their steadfast friendship had grown into a deep respect and love of a different kind. But still, Nate couldn't help but wish he'd done things differently in the beginning. Not rushed into anything new after Georgia left.

Stephanie had deserved more than that.

"She didn't think so."

That's because Jim didn't know the truth about that first pregnancy. No one else did, now that Stephanie was gone. Nate licked his lips. "I—"

Jim's phone rang on the side table. He picked it up and glanced at the screen. Frowned. "Excuse me, I need to take this."

"Sure."

"Hello?" Jim waited a moment while whoever was on the other line said something. Then he sat forward with a start and stood. "What? When?" Another pause. He glanced at Nate, frowned again. "I'll be right there."

"What is it?"

"That was Rosario, the church's night janitor. The church is flooding."

Together, they raced out into the rain, Nate nearly slipping on the wet grass between the parsonage and the church. Flinging open the front doors, they rushed into the sanctuary and halted at the sight in front of them. Water dripped down through the strung lights right onto the stage and pulpit area. The wood had already warped. Another leak had sprung all over the chairs and carpet in the center of the room, and a third ran down the walls between the sanctuary and exit to the kitchen area.

Rosario already had buckets out to catch more dripping, but it was as steady as the rain outside. "I'm sorry, Pastor. Nobody has been in here since we cleaned on Sunday, so we didn't know."

"Don't be sorry. This is my fault." Jim rubbed his forehead as he took in the damage. "The roof is likely the issue. It hasn't been replaced for…a while. It's been on my to-do list, but the coffers have been a bit low lately and it's a lot to spend." He turned to Nate. "Do you think your father's company would have time to fix this?"

"Maybe, but I'm not sure if it's possible to do before the holiday. I'll call Christian." He got on the phone with his cousin, but the results were less than ideal. Nate blew out a frustrated breath. "He says this rain has delayed their work on several projects, and he wouldn't be able to squeeze it in until after Christmas."

"That will certainly put a damper on the holiday, now won't it?" Jim paced. "I'd better call the insurance company. Maybe they can shed some light on what to do next. Rosario, we have some industrial fans out in the shed. Tarps too. Why don't the two of you call some friends to help get those over here and going?"

"On it." Nate shot off a text to Christian, who immediately said he'd be over with Malcolm Dunn and some others.

"Reinforcements are coming."

"Great. Meanwhile, I've got some calls to make. The insurance office is likely closed for the evening, but I'll see if I can get someone out here to assess our claim soon. That can put a delay on things too—and a lot of roofing companies are likely booked up for the next few weeks. I'm not optimistic we can get this handled before…" He pinned Nate with a pitying look.

"Before what?"

"The festival."

Nate stilled. He tasted bile. "No. That can't…" He took a deep breath. "We need that festival to help cover the youth center operating expenses."

"I know." Jim placed a hand on his shoulder and squeezed. "And I'm sorry again. But think of this as an opportunity to exercise that faith we were discussing earlier, hmm?"

"Easier said than done."

Maybe all of this was punishment. He didn't think God worked like that, but maybe it was his fault somehow. Maybe his lapse in judgment thirteen years ago—the ways he'd failed Stephanie, failed Georgia, failed himself—meant continued failure now.

No matter how hard he tried, he'd never be enough.

And Stephanie's dreams were going to die because of it.

Chapter Six

She was in her happy place.

Georgia hummed as she clicked to a new internet search for small-town festival ideas, browsing options and brainstorming from the comfort of Mimi's couch. She'd spent most of the last three days here—ever since her meeting with Nate on Sunday—enjoying the lit fireplace, rain pattering on the roof, and a constant infusion of coffee, courtesy of Mimi.

"You seem joyful tonight."

She glanced up to find her grandmother hovering, a purple porcelain mug in hand. "Hi."

"Hello, dear. Here." Mimi held the mug out to Georgia.

"Thank you." Shutting the laptop, Georgia placed it on the oak coffee table and took the mug from Mimi's outstretched hand. Mimi had started walking on her own Monday—baby steps to begin with—and the independence had seemed to reverse age her a bit. She already looked stronger and more capable. "And how do I seem joyful?"

Mimi lowered herself onto the faded floral-print couch. "You were humming."

"I was? Huh."

"Guess whatever you're doing is making you happy."

"I do love planning." Georgia took a sip of the coffee, a

new local brew she'd purchased at Caroline's shop. Mmm. Nice and strong, the way she liked it.

"Or maybe it's the man you're doing it for that's the source of the humming."

Georgia sputtered and pressed a hand to her mouth to wipe away a bit of stray coffee. "Don't be ridiculous."

"What's ridiculous about it? He's a handsome, generous man. You're a beautiful, whip-smart woman. And you loved each other, once upon a time."

The heat from the fireplace suddenly seemed like too much. "We may have said we loved each other, but we also hurt each other."

"You were teenagers. You've both changed since then."

"Still. I'm not sure that kind of hurt can be overcome, Mimi."

"Of course it can. It's called forgiveness, love. And if God can forgive us for every wrong we've ever done, then you can surely forgive Nate. And he can forgive you."

"I'm not so sure I did anything wrong." At Mimi's pointed look, she waved her hand through the air. "Fine, maybe I shouldn't have left without saying goodbye the night after begging him to go with me, and maybe I shouldn't have been so immature as to not have taken his calls. But I don't think he was too broken up about it. In the end, he moved on pretty quickly while I…"

"While you what?"

Georgia shrugged and pushed her thumb around the rim of her coffee mug. "Oh, just cried myself to sleep every night. My college roommate got so sick of it she started staying with her boyfriend just to get away from me. Meanwhile, Nate…"

"That boy was devastated for months."

"He had a funny way of showing it. Getting married half

a year later." She stared at the dark liquid in her cup. "You know, the ironic thing is that I was going to come back for him. I had spring break coming up, and I waffled for weeks on whether it was a good idea. But I was so miserable without him that I thought, oh, well. I'll just live with the consequences. Maybe we could try long distance, or maybe I could transfer schools to be closer to him. Go to the university in Flagstaff like I'd originally planned before Columbia offered me a spot. But then you told me he'd gotten married…"

"And you never came home again." Mimi squeezed her arm.

"I'm sorry for that. I should have. For you. It just…it hurt too much. And then, I threw myself into my studies. Into my work. I told myself it didn't matter, that I had done the right thing in leaving. And maybe I had." Georgia set her mug down on the side table and turned toward Mimi, who offered her a length of her quilt. Georgia took it and snuggled in beside her grandma like she was a kid again. "Because if I had never left, what would I have become? I'd have married him, Mimi. I'd have married him and been stuck in this town… always the drug addict's daughter. A nobody."

"You would have been my granddaughter. You would have been Nate's wife. And you would have been a daughter of the King. I don't think that's exactly a nobody."

"I didn't mean it like that. I'm proud to be your granddaughter."

"And yet, I'm the mother of a drug addict. By your account, I'm a nobody too."

Georgia sat up and faced Mimi, her jaw slack. "I didn't… that's not…"

Mimi patted her cheek. "People talk and judge what they don't know. They always will. They don't see how Brooke suffered after her daddy died. They don't see the many ways I failed to be there for her because of my own grief. How I spent more time nursing other people than my own daughter's broken spirit. How many times I have thought..." Mimi's soft smile wobbled. "But God has shown me that He knows, even when others don't. He knows our hearts, and His judgment is not based on the things we do. Or the things we fail to do."

"Then what's it based on?"

"His judgment, and his love for us, are both based on who we are to Him. His children. And just like I loved my Brooke until her last breath, no matter what she did, God loves us too. Our lives are significant because of Him. Because of His breath of life in us."

Georgia's eyes burned, and she looked away. Maybe she'd been doing all of this for the wrong reasons. "So you think I was wrong to leave all those years ago?"

"I think that the past cannot be changed. It's what we do now that matters. So whatever you do, big or small, do it as unto the Lord, Georgia-girl." Mimi struggled to her feet and, after a moment of standing there, turned to face Georgia again. "I *also* think that there is a very good man living next door who is now very much available and maybe deserves a second chance."

Then, as if she'd said nothing meaningful at all, Mimi shuffled toward the door.

"Wha—" Huffing, Georgia collected her mug and went after her grandma. "I don't want a second chance with Nate." She deposited the mug into the sink.

Mimi took a water cup and filled it from the spigot on the refrigerator door. "Your reasoning for not being with him again was because you'd hurt each other. If you can overcome that hurt, then what's stopping you?" She sipped on her water as innocent as could be.

What if...

No. Georgia shook her head. Love was not even on her radar right now. Maybe someday, when she'd settled into a director position. But not now, when she was on the brink of promotion. "There's also the little matter of me living in New York."

"And are you happy there, dear?"

"Of course I am. I've built a good life for myself."

"Okay." Mimi started to leave again, this time headed toward the hallway where her bedroom was located.

"Okay? That's all you have to say?"

Turning, Mimi winked. "I think I've said plenty for tonight. Good night, Georgia."

"Night." Georgia's head spun, and she got her own glass of water. Given the cup of coffee she'd just had, she wasn't anywhere near ready for bed, so she headed back into the living room to work on more of the festival plans. But when she got to her computer, her phone vibrated next to it.

A peek at the caller ID showed Nate's name. Why would he be calling this late? "Hello?"

"I need to talk to you." His voice sounded panicked and raw. "Are you home? Can you come over?"

"What's wrong? Is Cassie okay?" Georgia flew toward the door and stuffed her feet and pajama pants into her boots.

"What? Oh, yeah, Cassie's fine. She's finally sleeping though, so I can't come to your place. I'm sorry. You're probably busy. I just… I need to tell you something."

"You're scaring me." Flinging open the door, Georgia rushed out onto the porch. The rain had slowed, and the forecast showed clear weather for the rest of the week. "I'm coming. Hang on." She stuffed the phone into her pocket and ran toward his hunter green bungalow next door.

When she got to his door, he flung it open, letting her

in. She'd never been inside his place, though she'd caught a glimpse that day when she'd seen Cassie painting in the backyard. Was that only six days ago? It seemed a lifetime had occurred between then and now. She gave a quick glimpse at his living room—set up much the same way as Mimi's, with a TV and fireplace, a mantel with pictures of his late wife and daughter, a leather couch and recliner, and a noticeably bare nine-foot Christmas tree—before turning to the man himself.

He paced in front of the closed door. His hair stuck up in all directions like he'd been running his hands through it, and he wore a pair of jeans with mud splattered across the bottom and a button-down shirt that was half untucked and stained with what looked like mud too.

She'd never seen him look quite this…undone.

"Hey. What's going on?"

"The church. The roof. There was a massive leak." Nate kept pacing on the entryway tile, but his voice remained low—probably so as to not wake Cassie. "It flooded the sanctuary."

"Oh." Wait. *Oh*. "When will it be fixed?"

"Pastor Jim doesn't know." If Nate had been pacing on his carpet, there would be embers burning a hole in it by now. "The insurance company person he got ahold of said they can send someone out to inspect the damage on Monday—as in, not for five days—and after that they can see which of their approved contractors are available in the area. But with the holidays coming…"

Georgia swallowed. This wasn't good. "So the festival?"

Nate finally stopped pacing and looked her square in the eyes. "It's a no go. We either have to find another place to hold it, or not hold it at all. But we can't not hold it at all, or we won't get enough funding for the first year of operations.

But there's nowhere else in town with the capacity we need." He slumped back against the doorway. "I thought you might have some ideas. I know this isn't your fight, and this isn't what you signed on for, but I…"

Something deep inside of her hated seeing him like this. "Nate." Georgia took a step toward him.

"What am I going to do?"

Another step. Then another, until finally they were toe to toe. Then, without thinking of the consequences, Georgia slipped her arms around his torso and pressed her head to his chest. "It's going to be okay."

Nate's breath shuddered in, and his arms went around her too. His breathing evened out, matching hers, and she willed peace into him. And for just a moment, the past faded away. It didn't matter who had left who, or who had married who not long after. Right now, she was just a woman comforting a guy she still cared about.

The still caring part scared the living daylights out of her. But regardless, she stayed right where she was.

Finally, after what was probably too long, he whispered into her hair, "How have you always known how to calm me down?" Then, "Thank you, Georgia."

Her knees shook at the utter sweetness in his words, and the only thing she could do for her sanity was to pull away. To clear her throat and refocus. "You're welcome. And I meant what I said. It's going to be okay. We still have ten days to figure out a new location for this festival. And between your connections and my brains—" Georgia flipped her hair with a smile "—we'll have a new plan in no time."

"I don't know, Georgia. Maybe this is a sign."

"A sign of what?"

"First, there was the way Wayne ripped my business plan to shreds, and now this."

"When did he do that?" she asked.

"Monday night, at the town council meeting."

"Sorry, I didn't think to go and support you. I was buried under the planning."

"No, you used your time efficiently. Though maybe it doesn't matter after all, given what's happened at the church."

"The Nate Griggs I know isn't a quitter."

"I'm not trying to be a quitter. Just a realist."

"Okay, so think of this. *Realistically.*" Georgia cocked her head. "We *will* figure out the festival situation. And as far as the business plan goes, you do know I have an MBA right?" She pretended to crack her knuckles and swiveled her neck in an exaggerated stretch—first left, then right. "So let's get to work, Griggs. And I don't wanna hear another word about quitting."

That finally earned her a smile. "All right. You win."

Did she, though? Because the way she saw it, instead of being comfortably—and safely—tucked away on Mimi's couch alone all evening, she was spending it with the one guy who had ever truly broken her heart.

The guy Mimi thought deserved a second chance.

She'd done it. She'd really done it.

Not only had Georgia spent hours helping him whip the youth center's business plan into shape, but she'd found a location for the festival.

Nate shook his head as his truck rumbled up the hill toward The Lavender Farm at Pineberry Creek. Beside him, Georgia looked more than adorable in a puffy white jacket—with the rain had come some cooler weather they'd have to keep their eyes on—a purple beanie that made her brown eyes pop, jeans, and boots.

The same boots she'd worn with her blue snowflake pajamas on Wednesday night when she'd shown up and nearly bowled him over with that hug.

How had he forgotten how good Georgia Carrington felt in his arms?

Behind him, Cassie bounced in her booster, kicking the back of his seat and jabbering away to Georgia about all the fun things she wanted to do over Christmas break, which was rapidly approaching.

The tires of the truck popped over gravel on the section of Malcolm's graded lane that branched off Pineberry Creek Canyon Road, and he could hear the chunks of mud hitting the undercarriage.

"Do you think the road is going to be a problem?" Georgia asked during one of Cassie's rare pauses.

Nate gripped the wheel and went slow. The late afternoon light fell through the cracks of the trees onto the path. "Not usually. It's just because we've had so much rain and it's not paved. I didn't see any rain in the forecast this week, so fingers crossed."

"There's still the possibility of snow. That's the only thing that makes me nervous about an outdoor venue."

Yes. There was that. "What other choice do we have? Besides, the latest report on my app says there's less than a ten percent chance of flurries next weekend. I think we'll be okay." He side-glanced at Georgia, who was worrying her bottom lip.

Man, she was cute.

Not helpful, Nate.

He cleared his throat. "It was awesome of Malcolm to let us use his farm, especially free of charge. And so last minute."

"It was Taylor's idea. I also get the impression that a little extra publicity wouldn't hurt. He'd never say it, but I think he's had some trouble getting the farm profitable since buying it last year."

"That sounds like Malcolm." His buddy never asked for favors. "Guess it's a win-win for all of us, then."

The road curved slightly and opened up into a large acreage cleared of most trees and framed by the mountains in the background—and man, he'd never get tired of that view. At the end of the drive, Malcolm's log-style home abutted rows and rows of lavender, the leaves of which were a silvery, sage green color in their dormancy. There was another building where Malcolm worked on the lavender, and a small barn to house the goats and llamas, which also had a fenced-in enclosure for the animals to roam outside. Beyond that, there was an open area along Pineberry Creek that was covered with grass in the summertime.

Georgia leaned slightly forward in her seat. "Nate, it's perfect."

The awe in her voice made him chuckle as he pulled up beside the house and cut the ignition. "You should see this place in spring and summer. Those fields of lavender bloom with all varieties of purple and fragrant sweetness." They climbed out of the vehicle, and Cassie raced off, shouting about finding the goats.

Nate moved around the front of the truck to where Georgia stood. He pointed. "And see that open area down by the creek?"

She squinted. "Kind of."

"Malcolm set up a viewing bench so he can watch the elk and deer roaming the fields and mountains beyond."

"Gorgeous. I'm jealous Taylor gets to live here."

"Not for long, I hope," another voice said from the direction of the house.

They turned and Georgia rushed to give Taylor a hug.

Nate had grown up with Taylor and Malcolm, who were twins and every bit as different as two people could be. The other night at the church flooding, Malcolm had told Nate that something was going on emotionally with his sister—the way she'd moved home was so abrupt—but she wouldn't talk about it.

Nate waved and approached the front steps of the nineteen-hundreds-built farmhouse. "Hi, Taylor. Thanks again for suggesting this place."

"*Mi casa es su casa*—or in this case, Malcolm's home is your home." Taylor made a silly face, and Georgia laughed.

"Did you find a place of your own to move into?"

"Possibly. It's a junker, and Malcolm says I should just stay here, but…" Taylor shrugged. "I've got to stop looking to others to take care of me and start taking care of myself."

Georgia's forehead scrunched and she flicked a glance at Nate.

Before she could say anything, Taylor waved her hand around. "I saw Cassie run toward the goat pen—smart girl—so why don't you guys head there and I'll let Malcolm know you're here. You need anything to drink?"

"I'm good, thanks," Georgia said.

"Me too." After Taylor headed back inside, the front screen door closing with a *thwap*, Nate leaned closer to Georgia. "You think Taylor's okay?"

"I hope so." Georgia blinked at the front door for a long moment before shaking herself. "Okay, so I wanted to get your thoughts on everything I've got planned. Taylor sent over photos of the layout, but I still can't believe how perfect it is in person."

"Lead the way, oh, planner extraordinaire."

She shook her head at him and grinned. "I know I'm a

nerd when it comes to planning and execution, but this kind of thing just makes me happy."

"I like seeing you happy, Peach." The words—and old nickname—were out before he could think on them.

She sobered for a moment. "I like seeing you happy too."

They stared at each other until Cassie's far-off giggles broke the spell. Blinking fast, Georgia pressed her lips together and turned to face the open field. "So I'm thinking that down there along the creek is the perfect place to set up the booths and games. They'll be under a large white tent I ordered from an events company in Payson. It'll be available early next week—"

"That wasn't in the budget."

"Nate." She quirked an eyebrow at him. "I was *going* to say that in exchange for some advertising at the festival—a big banner they're supplying that says *Sponsored by Center Stage Events*—they offered it free of charge."

"Wow. I wouldn't have thought to ask for sponsorships."

"That's why you brought in the planner extraordinaire, right?" The grin she offered made him feel like one of the birds swooping and lifting again over the trees.

Lighter somehow.

Nauseated too.

"Right. Yeah. Sorry. I trust you, oh, great one."

"Let's not get carried away." Her laugh swirled behind her as she moved closer to the animal enclosure, where Cassie was currently surrounded by baby goats, Taylor squatting beside her. "Over there will be the gift-wrapping station, and past that, I'm thinking we'll set up photos with Santa and his reindeer."

"Reindeer?"

She pulled out a phone from her back pocket and swiped

open to a photo, which showed a dog wearing fake antlers on its head. "I figured it'll work for the goats and llamas."

"That's hilarious. Malcolm approved that?"

"Of course. Unlike some people, *he* trusts me."

"I trust you."

"Mm-hmm. Sure." She stuffed the phone back into her pocket. "Okay, over there we're going to have a few food trucks—"

"Couldn't stick with just one, huh?" He crossed his arms over his chest and gave her a look, but couldn't keep the smile off his face.

She smirked then kept walking. "No, we'll have three. Apple cider donuts and cider in one, a street taco truck—"

"Because nothing says Christmas like tacos." He hurried after her.

"You're impossible." Halting, she turned—and whoa, she was close. Reaching out to steady her, Nate almost stopped breathing at her nearness, at the scent of jasmine in her hair, at the way she blinked up at him with those round brown eyes full of surprise.

How did he always seem to find himself here, staring into her eyes and wanting to lean in…

To what? Kiss her? Confide in her? Find not just someone to hold, but to share his burdens with?

But it couldn't be like that with them again. Couldn't be the same, because *they* were different.

And as much as he liked teasing her, as soft as she might feel in his arms, as beautiful as she was, adult Georgia was still practically a stranger. There was still so much he didn't know about her, about her life.

About why she'd left like she did all those years ago. Why she'd devastated him.

And after the festival next weekend, she'd be gone again.

Besides, between his upcoming career change, the weight of his family's expectations, and Cassie, Nate had way too much on his plate as it was. So there really wasn't much point in entertaining romantic thoughts—or nostalgic memories—about Georgia in any way, shape, or form. It was foolishness, pure and simple.

What was the saying? *Fool me once, shame on you. Fool me twice...shame on me.*

And Nate wouldn't be the fool again.

Nate took a step back and forced a smile. "Should we go get in some baby goat snuggles with Cassie?"

Georgia looked visibly shaken, but she flicked on a smile too. "Sure. Yes. Great idea."

And they headed that way, together but separate...a wise move.

Even if a very small—very illogical—part of him wished things *could* be different this time.

Chapter Seven

He'd almost kissed her.

At least, she thought so.

Even more than an hour later, the truth still shook Georgia. She stood alone down by the creek, its water burbling over stones as it passed tranquilly by. The sun had started its descent, burnishing the mountains a gorgeous orange and yellow. Down the creek a ways, a mama elk and its child drank from the water.

Her surroundings were perfectly peaceful—a direct contrast to the tightness in her chest.

Gravel crunched under someone's feet to her right, and she turned to find Taylor walking the path that led from the house down this way. Her skin was pale, and her hair pulled up in a messy bun. "There you are. Nate said you were doing some final checks for the festival, but it looks like something else might be on your mind."

"What? No. Just excited about how perfect this place is."

Taylor tugged her colorful woven shawl tighter around her shoulders. "Look, I know we just reconnected, and maybe you don't trust me yet, but we were good friends once, G. So don't try to pretend with me. This isn't your corporate office where you have to tuck your emotions away. It's okay to have feelings about the fact that your ex nearly kissed you—and that, from where I was standing, it seemed like you might have wanted him to."

Georgia's stomach twisted and she tugged on the edges of her beanie right over her ears, groaning. "I did. I did want him to. At least, in that moment."

And that had shaken her too. Because she should be stronger than that. More sensible. But this place… Pineberry… it had a way of drawing her in. Reminding her of the girl she'd once been.

It was a strange sort of dissonance. The remembering. The longing.

Accompanied by the desire to forget.

Her friend came closer and stood beside Georgia. "That's what I thought." Taylor's five-eleven frame dwarfed Georgia's five-two, but there was something comforting in it—even if she'd always been the brutally honest one.

"For the record, it has nothing to do with not trusting you. I think I've just gotten out of practice with sharing my heart, you know?"

"Is that why you begged off of girls' night yesterday? Too afraid we'd pry?"

"What? No, of course not. I've just had a lot going on with the festival planning."

"That's what I figured, but you know Caroline. She's more sensitive than me."

Great. "The last thing in the world I'd ever want to do is hurt Caroline. Or you."

"Eh, don't worry about me. I'm tough. I know it's a dog-eat-dog world out there. I lived in Los Angeles." Taylor's hand rested absently on her stomach. "Of course, it chewed me up and spit me out, and now I'm living with the consequences of my own decisions, so that didn't work out so well for me. I think maybe Caroline was the smart one, staying in Pineberry all these years."

"I kind of want to ask what happened to you, but that feels hypocritical knowing I haven't really told you much about my life in New York."

"We're both works in progress, right? And I will tell you what's going on with me. Just not yet. Suffice it to say I've made a mess of my life, but I've finally come back to the Lord and I'm learning...well, a lot," Taylor said. "Mostly that I have to be honest with myself. And you have to be honest with yourself too. What are you feeling with Nate? Is it love? Is it just nostalgia?"

"Definitely not love." At Taylor's pointed look, Georgia sighed. "Fine. I don't know what I'm feeling. I've gotten good at stuffing my emotions down. They're not super useful in the corporate world, and that's been my life for the last decade."

"Makes sense. But there's nothing stopping you from exploring your emotions now."

"What's the point? I'm leaving in a little over a week."

"But you don't want to regret not using your time here well."

"I'm using it well. Planning this festival. Spending time with Mimi."

"True. But maybe this is also a chance to find a bit of closure."

The sun dipped fully behind the mountains, and the stars were finally allowed to shine. The moon too...and it was full. Beautiful.

"I don't need closure. I'm fine."

"Uh-huh."

And this was why she mostly stuck to herself in New York. No pesky friends digging to the heart of matters and stirring up trouble. Except, it was nice—having someone care. "All right, I can admit that perhaps my emotional growth has been a bit...stunted."

"And?"

Georgia couldn't help but smile at the singsong tone of Taylor's voice. "And, maybe closure wouldn't be a bad thing." She sighed. "I'd just have no idea where to start."

"You don't have to have a whole plan. Just feel your way through it."

"Feelings are what got me in this mess in the first place."

"No. It was running away from those feelings that landed you where you are today."

"Ouch." Georgia shook her hand as if Taylor had stung it. "You're really flinging those truth bombs tonight, huh?"

Taylor nudged her with an elbow. "Speak the truth in love and all that."

Another crunch of boots sounded behind them, and they both turned to find Nate walking down the path, clutching two mugs and a blanket under his arm.

"And as for not knowing where to start...well, at the very least, you should tell him why you left like you did if you haven't already. You owe him—and yourself—that much."

Taylor squeezed Georgia's elbow and sauntered back up the path, stopping to say something to Nate before continuing back to the house.

Nate approached. "I didn't mean to scare her away. Brought you ladies some hot chocolate." He extended one of the travel mugs to her. "Guess this other one's for me now."

"Thanks." She took the offered drink. "I didn't mean to delay us. Do we need to get going?"

"Nah, it's a Saturday night and Cassie is having a blast. Malcolm has three dogs and she's in absolute heaven. He invited us to stay for dinner if you'd like."

"Oh, sure. If you want to. If not, we can head home. Mimi is planning dinner with Elizabeth tonight since I wasn't sure when we'd be back."

"Cool." He pulled out his phone and his fingers flew across the screen, then pocketed it again. "Just told him to throw a steak on for each of us."

"Great."

Nate glanced behind Georgia. "Would you like to sit while they cook, or go back to the house?"

Taylor's words resonated inside Georgia's mind. "We can sit."

Together, they walked to the wooden bench and settled back against it. Nate draped the blanket over Georgia's lap.

She looked up at him. "We can share. If you're cold."

"Okay. Thanks." He scooted a little closer and tugged the edge of the blanket over him. Their thighs weren't even touching, but she could still feel his warmth. "I came up here right after Mal bought the place last year, but not much since. It sure is pretty. You remember coming out here for our sixth grade field trip?"

She laughed and tested her hot chocolate. Warm, sweet, and decadent with only a few marshmallows—just the way she liked it. "I seem to remember a few of you reckless boys daring each other to stand in the freezing-cold creek with your shoes off to see who could last the longest."

"I won." Nate grinned and took a sip of his cocoa. "And for the record, we weren't reckless. We were trying to impress the ladies with our bravery."

"Impress the ladies? You were twelve."

"It has to start somewhere. And it never stops."

"Oh, yeah? You'd strip off your boots and socks and go stand in the creek to impress some girls now?"

"Nah, I've gotten way more sophisticated. Now I just

bring them hot chocolate and blankets and rope them into helping me with holiday festivals."

That made her chuckle. "Ah, I see. Well, color me impressed."

"There was a time when I'd have done anything to impress you, Georgia."

And that's when the teasing stopped, and things got real. Silence fell around them other than the sound of the wind rustling through plants that were dead—that would someday come back to life.

Georgia didn't know if that would ever happen for her and Nate, but Taylor was right. He deserved to hear the truth. And an apology. "Nate, I'm sorry I left like I did. Thirteen years ago, I mean."

His thumb flinched against his mug, and his Adam's apple bobbed. A few silent moments, and then, "Why did you?"

How could she tell him without hurting him? But maybe it went back further than that moment. "It was never just about you. I want you to know that."

"How could it not be?"

What had Taylor said? That she should just feel her way through this? Georgia pressed her lips together before unlocking the memories—and diving into them.

"I had a conversation with my mom when I was nine, the night before she overdosed." She stared at the creek, how it distorted the moon's light as the water ran over pebbles and stones. "You know how I told you she was a painter? How she'd wanted to go to school for that? She'd been painting in our tiny apartment in Dallas, and I came up behind her and complimented her on her artwork. Instead of thanking me, she started sobbing. She tore the canvas off the easel and broke it over a lamp, screaming about how it was all my dad's fault that she was in this 'mess'—aka, a single mom at the age of twenty-six with a deadbeat waitress job scraping together enough money to make ends meet. And addicted to drugs too, though I didn't realize that at the time. I just knew she was sick a lot. Slept a lot."

Nate's hand drifted toward hers. He snagged it and squeezed before releasing his hold.

She almost wished he hadn't let go. But it was better—so she wouldn't let herself get confused.

This was about closure. Nothing more.

"That night, she told me that my dad had tricked her. That he'd said he loved her, that he'd provide for her, and she gave up her life here in Pineberry to chase him, to chase his dreams of being a musician. But when she got pregnant, he left. See, she was going to be somebody, but then, because of a man…"

His forehead furrowed, Nate cleared his throat and took another drink of cocoa, but didn't say anything.

"All of that to say, when I moved here, everyone looked at me as the drug addict's daughter. And I wanted to be more than that. I wanted to be somebody too." She studied Nate in the moonlight. He was just as handsome in a shadowy light as in a brilliant one. And his eyes pierced hers with conviction…like he had something to say, but was waiting for her to finish. "That's why I left. Because my dream had always been to go Ivy League. And when that spot at Columbia came through at the last minute, with a scholarship to boot, the state university in Flagstaff just wasn't going to cut it. I had to go."

"I understand that. But why not say goodbye? Why cut me out of your life completely? That was the worst part."

"Because I knew how much I loved you, Nate. And when I asked you to come with me, and you told me you had to stay here, to take over your family's business one day, I was afraid you would ask me to stay if I came to say goodbye. I didn't think I was strong enough to resist that. But I *did* know I had to get out of here, to be somebody. Does that make sense?" she asked. "But I am sorry. It was wrong not to say goodbye. To never speak to you again."

He brushed his thumb up and over the edge of his mug's lid, then back down. "Maybe I should have considered going with you instead of defaulting to pleasing my family. I just couldn't fathom saying no to them. Not after…"

"After what?"

He huffed a laugh. "Seems both of our childhoods left a few scars."

"How so?"

"My mom's dad used to live in Pineberry. He passed a few years after you moved to town."

"I think I remember him." He'd been large, grizzled, and kind of brash, if she recalled correctly.

"He and I were really close until I was about ten or eleven. Gramps was a huge fisherman and we used to go fishing together a lot, until I got more into sports. One time we had a fishing trip planned, but my basketball team ended up having an extra game that same weekend—the last of the season. I wanted to be there for my team and play, but Gramps… well, he wanted to fish. Said it was good fishing that weekend, and if I didn't want to go, he'd take Christian instead. So he did. After that, he never asked me to go again, and all but ignored me."

"Oh no. Nate, that's awful."

Nate offered a small grin-and-bear-it smile. "When I asked Mom why Gramps was treating me like that, she said, 'Would *you* really want to spend time with someone who chose a silly game over time with you? No, you wouldn't, and neither does your grandpa. I can't say that I blame him for finding a new favorite.'"

"I'm sorry, what? She did not say that!"

"She was just trying to help me understand, I guess."

"Understand what?"

He shrugged. "That sometimes keeping the peace is more important than getting what you want."

"That's so manipulative."

"What? How?"

"You were a child, and your adult grandfather shouldn't have punished you for that. Besides, you're allowed to say no to somebody and not worry about losing their love."

"Of course." He shifted on the seat, frowned. "Although when I didn't do what you wanted, I lost your love."

The truth smacked her in the gut. She set her mug on the ground and turned on the bench to fully face Nate. "I'm so sorry, Nate. In my desire to make something of myself, I made you feel like nobody. But you were never a nobody to me. You were…everything. And to be honest, that scared me."

"You were always a somebody to me too, Peach. And while we're being honest, our bond has always scared me also. The worst thing I could imagine was losing you. And then…it happened." His eyes searched hers. "I don't think I could take it happening again."

She sucked in a breath. What did he mean? It *wouldn't* happen again, because he wasn't her somebody anymore, and she wasn't his.

And yet…

Maybe this was about more than closure, after all. Maybe, somehow, they could find their way back to each other. Not romantically, of course—that would never work. But how could she hate the idea of this kind, generous man being part of her life? That was immature, limited, and Georgia was determined to grow emotionally, after all.

Taylor would be proud.

Georgia tipped her chin upward. "It's a good thing you don't ever have to lose me again. Because I may have disappeared on you before, but we're friends now, Nate. Which means, whether I'm in New York or back here visiting Mimi, you and Cassie are stuck with me for life."

"Is that what we are, Georgia? Friends?"

Could she really do that? Be friends with this man who had hurt her so profoundly by not choosing her? But when she looked in her heart, the unwillingness to forgive that she'd carried around like an anchor…it wasn't there. Maybe some fear and uncertainty, some tenderness, still lingered, but the bitterness had fled.

"Yes. Friends."

Nate finally cleared his throat, ducking his head. "Thanks for including Cassie in that statement. She seems really taken by you. Not that I blame her." He frowned. "She's just had so much loss lately. And I'm trying, but there's work and the youth center and just life…"

"You're doing a great job, Nate."

"It just doesn't feel like enough." His eyes found hers again. "I keep getting things wrong. But you're just so naturally good with her."

"She's an easy kid to love." Georgia's heart squeezed with the truth of that statement. "You know, I've been so busy building my career over the last decade that I haven't stopped to think much about having my own kids. But something about Cassie…from day one, she's just drawn me in. Made me feel like part of something. That's really rare."

"I think she feels a connection to you because you lost your mom when you were a kid too. You know how it feels."

Georgia thought back to what Cassie had told her last week in the backyard. "Nate."

"Yeah?"

She chewed the inside of her lip. Was she overstepping? But they were friends now, and friends told each other the truth. "Cassie doesn't think you miss Stephanie."

"What?" Nate sat back abruptly, his elbow knocking against the bench's arm. His forehead furrowed, and he rubbed his arm. "Why would she say that? Of course I miss her."

"She said you never cry or talk about her."

"I never..." He ran a hand across his head, gripping his hair in his fist. It would have been adorable if it wasn't also heartbreaking. "Of course I've cried. Of course I miss her. She was my best friend. She was there for me when..." He looked away. "We saw each other through a lot. How could I not miss her?"

"Of course you do." Georgia's eyes burned and her heart ached for him. For all he'd lost. "But Cassie is a child, and she doesn't see all of that. How can she, if you don't show her?"

"I need to be strong for her." Elbows balanced on his knees, Nate leaned forward. His folded hands rested against his mouth as he stared out at the creek.

"And you are. You're amazing." Reaching a hand toward him, Georgia set it lightly on his back and rubbed circles of comfort there. "But Cassie needs permission to process, to grieve. If you're pretending everything's okay, it doesn't give her that permission. It signals to her that we don't talk about this. We ignore it. We stuff it away. And maybe that works for a while, but sooner or later, it comes out."

"Did that happen for you?"

"Thankfully, Mimi talked about Mom all the time. She asked me what I missed most about her. She'd tell me funny stories of when she was a kid. She'd set up easels in the living room and we'd paint portraits in memory of Mom, even though we were both terrible." Georgia smiled at the memories. "It wasn't until I was a little older that I started hearing the rumors about how Mom really died. As a kid, I didn't understand that she'd overdosed. I just thought she'd gotten sick and died in her sleep, you know? Turned out, it was more complicated than that."

Turned out, Brooke Carrington had chosen drugs and numbness over her own daughter.

But that wasn't the point of this conversation.

"I'm glad you had that." Nate glanced over his shoulder at her. "I want that for Cassie too. I'm just not sure how."

A thought struck Georgia. "Care for a suggestion?"

"I'm all ears."

"Good. What are you doing tomorrow night?"

This was either the most foolish thing Nate had ever done...or the most brilliant.

But if it helped Cassie—if it made her smile—then nothing else mattered.

He opened his front door to find Georgia on the stoop. She wore those adorable pajamas again and her hair was pulled back in a graceful ponytail. Over her arm was slung a bag that looked quite full, and in her hands she had a platter of Christmas cookies. "Hi," she said, all smiles. No reservations.

"Hi, yourself. Let me help you with that."

She let him take the platter and stepped inside. "Thanks." Then she scanned the living room and glanced down the hallway. "Where's Cassie?"

"I told her to go change into her favorite pajamas. She called me a *silly daddy*, but ran off to obey."

"Speaking of pajamas—" she ran her finger up and down through the air, indicating the flannel pajama pants and white T-shirt Nate wore "—looking good there, Mr. Mayor."

He chuckled. "Couldn't have anyone accuse me that I didn't go all out for this pajama party." Closing the door behind Georgia, Nate headed to the kitchen island right behind the couch and set the platter of cookies beside the big bowl of popcorn he'd made and the half-empty box of pizza he and Cassie had consumed for their Sunday evening dinner. "And I spent the afternoon dragging all the decorations out of the attic while Cassie had some quiet time in her room. They're in the garage if you want to help me pull them inside."

"Perfect." Georgia set the bulging bag on one of his kitchen stools, patting it. "And in here I've got all the Christmas classics I could scrounge up on DVD. We can let Cassie choose what to watch once we've decorated."

"Awesome." Nate led Georgia into the tiny garage space stuffed to the brim with boxes—no room for a vehicle, which was why he parked in the driveway. He flicked on a light and pointed to the two large green tubs he hadn't seen since before Stephanie died. "There. I already cleaned the dust off them." Then he paused. "We're doing the right thing, yeah? I don't want to rewrite Cassie's memories with Stephanie."

"You'll never do that, Nate. She will always have those memories." Georgia smiled at him, sweet and reassuring. In the small space, her jasmine scent wrapped itself around him and squeezed him like an embrace. "It's time for her to make new ones, and to share something that was special between the two of them with others. With us. I'm just happy you're letting me be part of it."

"Are you kidding? It was your idea. And you know how to talk to her about this stuff."

"You do too, Nate. Just take the pressure off and enjoy yourself."

"Thanks, Georgia." He indicated the nearest tub. "You lift one handle and I'll lift the other?"

She saluted. "Aye, aye, Captain." Her eyes sparkled as she laughed and took hold of one side.

Before they could figure out who was going to open the heavy door, it was flung wide. "Daddy, what are you doing— Georgia?" Cassie squealed and ran out to hug Georgia, who let go of the handle and threw her arms around Nate's daughter.

The sight pummeled Nate in the stomach. A twisting— warm but also painful.

Then Cassie stepped back and looked Georgia up and down. "Are you in your pj's too?"

"I am." Georgia spun around like she was on a runway, showing off the bright pants and Henley-type shirt that hugged her curves. "What do you think?"

"I think you look comfy like me." Cassie peeked around her. "What's in the tubs?"

Georgia booped her on the nose. "Let us bring them inside and you'll see. Can you grab the door for us?"

"Yeah!" Cassie bounced back to open the door, leaning back against it to make way for Nate and Georgia as they hauled the first box inside. "Can I open it now?"

Nate laughed and ruffled her hair. "Go ahead."

She needed a little help with the latch, but when she got the lid off, Cassie just stood there staring at the decorations for a moment. Nestled on top were the family stockings, and Cassie lifted out Stephanie's silver one decorated with glitter and sequins. Her bottom lip trembled and she looked up at Nate with tears in her eyes. Oh no.

"You okay, honey?"

"Are we decorating with Mommy's stuff?"

Nate gave Georgia a quick look, and she must have recognized the panic in his eyes. She gave a gentle nod. He inhaled a deep breath, then kneeled in front of the box and his daughter. "Georgia and I thought you might like that, but if it makes you too sad, we don't have to."

"No, I want to. Thank you, Daddy." Cassie crashed into Nate and he fell back onto his rear, holding his daughter on the rug as she cried.

A tear crested down his face too.

Cassie glanced up at him and lifted her hand to his cheek, pressing her palm against his tear. "It's okay, Daddy. You don't have to worry. Mommy's in Heaven."

Behind Cassie, Georgia sat on the couch and swiped tears from her own eyes.

Nate refocused on the precious girl in his arms. The one he'd failed so much, but who loved and forgave him for it anyway. "I know, honey." He hugged her back to him and took a shuddering breath. "I'm crying because I miss her."

"You do?" she mumbled into his chest.

"I really do. But you know what?"

She lifted her head again. "What?"

"She would be so incredibly proud of you. Her little bird."

"She used to call me that. Why?"

He smoothed her hair back. "Because you always bring the sweetest music wherever you go." Nate pressed his nose against hers. "And because you chatter on like a little magpie who's never met a stranger."

Cassie giggled. "I guess that's true."

"Oh, it's definitely true," Georgia said from her spot on the couch. "You were the first one to welcome me back to Pineberry."

"Yeah, because Daddy wasn't doing such a good job, huh?"

"Hey, now!" Nate started to tickle Cassie, making her squeal and wriggle away, running toward the couch and leaping up behind Georgia, using her as a shield.

"She's right, you know." Georgia's eyes flashed with teasing before she turned over her shoulder to speak to Cassie. "I thought your daddy was the police come to arrest me. Turns out, it was just the mayor on a power trip."

That set Cassie off giggling again, and she fell into Georgia's arms laughing.

Oh, his heart. He could sit here and watch the two of them all night. Especially with the way Georgia had finally opened up to him last night—the way she'd apologized right before declaring them friends again—he wanted her to feel like part of something here.

He stood and lightly kicked the green tub. "You ladies ready to stop making fun of me and get some Christmas decorations up?"

Cassie cheered. "Yes!" She leaped from the couch onto the ground and started pulling more decor out from the box while Georgia and Nate headed to the garage to get the other tub.

When they were alone, he turned to Georgia, took her hand. The feel of her softness against his rough-worn fingers was almost too good. Too much to even hope for. "Thank you," he said, allowing one swipe of his thumb across her knuckles.

She visibly swallowed. "For what?"

"For helping me connect with my daughter."

"I didn't do anything."

"Don't do that—don't discount your value in this." His tone came out huskier than intended. But why couldn't she see herself the way he'd always seen her? "Don't discount your value to me. To us."

"Okay." She pressed her lips together. "But don't discount your own value either. Do you make mistakes? Sure. Are you going to have some trouble navigating some major events in your daughter's life? Of course—especially this. But you're a good dad, Nate. You care. And that is a thousand times more than I ever got in a father. Cassie is blessed beyond measure to have you supporting her and taking care of her."

Aw, Georgia. "Your dad is probably kicking himself for missing out on the greatest thing he ever had in his life."

She gave a sad smile. "I sincerely doubt that."

"Then I feel sorry for him." Nate let go of her and grabbed the green tub with both hands. "Can you get the door?"

Georgia blinked at him for a moment, then scurried to open it. "Here."

They headed back to the living room, where Cassie already had a box of handmade ornaments out and laid in a row. Georgia grabbed her phone and turned on some Christmas music, starting with "Rockin' Around the Christmas Tree."

Then she oohed and aahed over the ornaments. "Tell me about each one."

"I made that one for Mommy when I was in preschool. And that one has a picture of when Mommy and Daddy took me to see Santa for the first time." Cassie lowered her voice to a whisper. "I was kind of scared but didn't want them to know, so I sat on his lap anyway. And Mommy told me how brave I was after."

Nate grabbed the fishing line and needle he'd prepped earlier today, plus the bowl of popcorn. He sat on the couch and started to string the popcorn one piece at a time onto the line, listening while Cassie told story after story of Stephanie. Georgia turned to him and prompted him with questions about his wife, and that led to some great reminiscing.

As Georgia lifted her up to set ornaments in the higher branches of the tree, Cassie was enthralled with the story of an elementary school Stephanie playing an angel in the church's Christmas pageant, while Nate had been the mean innkeeper. And the memory of their first Christmas with Cassie as a newborn baby—just a month old—when they wrapped her in blankets and took her out to stargaze and it had started to snow.

"Christmas was your mom's favorite time of year." Nate finished up the popcorn garland and carried it to the tree, which was already heavy with decorations. He fed one end into Georgia's hands and together, they wrapped the strand around the tree. Their fingers brushed against each other with every pass through the branches. "She said it was when she felt closest to God."

"I like that," Cassie said. "And now, it helps me feel closest to Mommy too."

"I'm so glad, honey." Nate turned to find her holding the final ornament—a baby Jesus in a porcelain manger. "You want to hang that up high?"

She nodded, and he hefted her up onto his shoulder. Georgia stood beside them, quiet, lending her support without saying a word, while Cassie leaned forward and placed the ornament on the tree. He stepped back, Cassie's arms around his neck, and Georgia stepped back with them. He couldn't help but slip his arm through hers, and she leaned her head against him—well, against Cassie's leg—as they took in the moment, "Silent Night" playing appropriately in the background.

It didn't matter the particulars. This was a memory he'd never forget.

The song was interrupted by a buzzing, and Georgia jumped. "Oh! Sorry." She walked toward her phone and picked it up, frowning. "It's my boss. I'd better get this."

"Absolutely, go ahead." Nate lowered Cassie to the ground.

"Hello?" Georgia said, turning away.

Heading toward the kitchen, Nate grabbed the bag Georgia had brought over and lowered it to the wooden floor toward Cassie. "Here, why don't you pick out a movie for us to watch?"

"Oh, goody!" Cassie eyed the platter of cookies. "Will we get some dessert while we watch?"

"I believe that's why Ms. Frances and Georgia made them, silly."

Making a face, Cassie sat on the floor and pulled DVDs with bright red and green on their cases from the bag.

"What?" Georgia's voice peaked.

Nate didn't want to eavesdrop, but the room was small, and if Georgia had wanted total privacy, she'd have gone out on the porch or down the hallway. Snatching a cookie from underneath the cellophane, Nate turned toward Georgia and leaned back against the island counter.

She was frowning, tugging on the ends of her hair the way she did whenever she was worried or nervous.

What was this all about?

Georgia's eyes snapped up to meet his, and there was an apology in them. Then she looked back toward the fireplace and mumbled a few things into the phone that he couldn't catch before hanging up. She remained looking away from him.

Finishing off the cookie—which he'd barely tasted—Nate eased himself off the counter and walked toward her. When he reached her side, he stuck his hands into his pockets. "Everything okay?"

"No." Her voice shook. "My boss said…ugh."

"Hey." He turned to her, cupped her elbow. "What is it?"

"Nate, I'm so sorry, but…" She bit her lip. "My boss said the interviews for my promotion—which were supposed to be the twenty-third—have now been moved up to the seventeenth."

"What? But that's…"

"Three days from now. I know."

Yes, three days from now.

And three days *before* the festival.

Chapter Eight

True friends came when you texted an SOS—even if it that text was sent at four in the morning on a Monday.

Three hours later, Georgia pulled into Malcolm Dunn's driveway and climbed from her vehicle into the early morning chill. Fog hung on the outer recesses of the lavender farm, and the first light of day peeked over the mountains.

As she grabbed her briefcase and shut her door, Caroline's Jeep rumbled up behind her. Georgia tugged her jacket tight as she waited for her friend to park. A simple knit blue beanie tugged down around her ears and a bleary look in her eyes, Caroline wore her brown hair back in a low ponytail, a pair of worn jeans, and a bulky sweatshirt along with a pair of sneakers.

Georgia's throat swelled. Would anyone in her life back in New York show up like this—without an explanation necessary?

"Thank you so much for coming last minute." Georgia pulled Caroline into a hug. Her friend smelled like warm vanilla.

"It sounded important." Caroline pulled back, her eyes rimmed in worry. "Is everything okay?"

"Um." Georgia's fingers clung to the strap of her briefcase. "Not exactly. I'll tell you inside."

They started toward the house, where the lights glowed as warm from the inside as those strung along the roof on the outside.

"I hope this doesn't interfere with your shop opening on time today," Georgia said as they climbed the front porch steps.

"It's not like a few extra hours will help me stay in the black any better."

Georgia halted their progress. "The shop is struggling?" Why hadn't Caroline said anything? Not that Georgia had spent much time with her old friend. She'd visited her once, maybe twice, but they'd largely ended up talking about Georgia and her life in New York. Then, she'd gotten busy with festival planning.

And now that she was leaving again, she wouldn't have the time to delve deeper with Caroline, or Taylor either.

She was a terrible friend.

Caroline shrugged. "Mom was always the businesswoman, the brains behind the operations. But once her dementia set in…" She looked away, inhaled a breath. "And now that I'm operating the shop alone and paying the bills for her assisted living facility too…it's just a lot."

Oh, Caroline. "I'm so sorry, Care. I didn't know."

"How could you?" Her friend's words were soft. No censure. No judgment.

But Georgia couldn't let herself off the hook so easily. "I should have known. Just like I should have known about Mimi's surgery. If I'd been here…"

"Hey." Caroline looped her arm through Georgia's. "You're here now."

Her words were a knife through Georgia's already shredded chest. Because ever since Bob's call last night—ever since having to tell Nate she was leaving early, seeing the disappointment in his eyes, not being able to sleep—she'd felt like half a person. And for the first time, she wished she could be in two places at once.

The front door opened, and Taylor's brother, Malcolm, stepped out in his Wranglers, brown cotton duck jacket, and the Stetson he'd never been without the few times Georgia had seen him about town and on Saturday when he'd grilled them up the most delicious steak she'd ever eaten.

He pulled up short when he saw the two women on his porch. A frown made deep grooves in his well-cut cheeks. "What's going on here?"

"Well, good morning to you too, Mr. Grumpy Pants." Caroline bounced up the last few steps and flicked his hat upward so the brim pointed skyward.

"You know what's usually good about morning?" Malcolm popped the hat back down, no amusement in his eyes. "The peace and quiet." Before they could answer, he maneuvered around them and headed for the barn.

Caroline placed a hand on her hip and shook her head at his retreating back. "One of these days I'm going to get that man to smile."

"Is he always like that? The Malcolm I remember from high school was quiet, much more solemn than the others, but he joked around with the boys too."

"He changed when his parents died." Caroline leaned against the front porch post. "And I get it—it was a terrible tragedy."

"Tragedies do have a way of changing us."

"But they don't have to. We can still be happy—find joy—even in the terrible things."

Ah, Caroline. Always the optimist. "That's something I admire about you. It's harder for the rest of us mere mortals."

"Whatever." Caroline opened the front door. "Come on. Let's find Tay."

They both entered the house's living room—worn furniture covered with quilts, a mounted deer rack, and a rustic log-and-brick fireplace—then made their way into the kitchen, where Taylor stood in front of a coffee maker in an oversized hot pink sweater, pajama pants, and slouchy socks.

When she saw them, her eyes brightened, and she rushed to give hugs. "I've been worried. What's going on?"

"Wow, no hello first, huh?" Georgia tried for a tease, but the concern in Tay's voice nearly drove her to tears.

She'd cried—or almost cried—more in the last two weeks than in the last thirteen years combined. What was wrong with her?

"Fine. Hello." Taylor popped a hand on her hip. "Now sit down and tell us what's going on."

"First, coffee." Caroline waved her hand at the coffeepot. "Please."

"Okay, but I warn you—Malcolm's machine is ancient. Thankfully the local beans you sold me are amazing. But don't blame me if there's still something lacking. I told him he needs a better machine—something from this century, preferably—and he said he takes it black and this is good enough for him."

"That man." Caroline laughed.

Taylor padded over to the machine and removed the pot from the brewing station, pouring a stream of steaming liquid into an oversized mug, which she handed to Caroline. "You want some, G?"

"Sure." Georgia removed her jacket and slung it over one of the kitchen barstools. "Thanks."

After Taylor poured drinks for herself and Georgia, they all sat at the breakfast nook, where a bank of huge windows showed off the mountains in the distance. The chipped oak table had seen better days, but was sturdy and strong. With a little sanding and a new coat of stain, this thing would have many years of life left.

Georgia wrapped her hands around the mug, allowing its warmth to infuse her with strength. "Last night I was helping Nate and Cassie decorate their house for Christmas—"

"I'm sorry, what?" Caroline's palm pressed into her chest. "That's adorable. How was it?"

"Good. Really good, actually." Georgia smiled at the memory. "Cassie was amazingly sweet, and Nate was so great with her. It was something she and Stephanie always did together, and so we weren't sure how she'd react. But then we started sharing memories of her mom with her, and I think it was just really cathartic and good for them."

Taylor and Caroline exchanged a look.

Georgia's eyes narrowed. "What?"

"What do you mean, *what*?" Taylor's eyebrows arched over her mug as she took a sip—her eyes all innocence.

Uh-huh. Georgia pointed between the two of them. "What was that look?"

Caroline flicked another look Taylor's way, this one a bit apprehensive. Then she focused on Georgia again. "It just sounds like you and Nate…"

"Are maybe *you and Nate* again," Taylor finished.

"What? No. We're just friends." Both of her friends silently drank their coffee at the same time, but their nonresponses echoed loudly in the room. "We *are*."

"No, we *totally* believe you," Taylor said. "But back to sharing memories of Stephanie—how did that make you feel?"

"It was fine." Georgia's fingers flexed against the smooth ceramic surface of her mug. "Why wouldn't it be?"

"Maybe because she's the woman he turned to after you left."

"It's in the past. Besides, like I said…we're just friends."

"Yeah, but Georgia…" Caroline reached across the table for Georgia's arm, patting it. "I know how hurt you were. So hurt you never came back home."

"I shouldn't have let that keep me away. And yeah, it hurt, but I'm over it now. It's not like I can be jealous anymore. She was his wife. I never was. She belonged to him in a way I never did." Coffee burned down her throat as she took a long draught. "What kind of woman would be jealous of someone who's gone? That's absurd. And immature."

"Matters of the heart are never easy. And they don't always make sense. Sometimes, emotions blind us to the truth." Taylor shifted in her chair. "Regardless of what your head says, with how much you loved Nate, you'd have to be a complete robot if thinking about Stephanie didn't cause at least some pain. Remember what I said about being honest with yourself?"

Georgia blinked, allowing herself to identify her tangle of emotions. She inhaled a shaky breath. "Okay. Yes, thinking about her is painful—though after last night, it's mostly pain for Cassie and Nate. To lose your spouse and mom… well, I know at least half of that pain. And as far as me and Nate goes, I think the pain is less about Stephanie herself and more about the question of *what if*. What if I'd come home right away? What if I'd never left? Where would we be now if I'd chosen differently back then? Then again, maybe he was always meant to be with Stephanie. Maybe I had to move aside so he could find her."

And oh, how that thought raked her insides across imaginary coals.

It shouldn't. But it did.

Caroline squeezed her arm. "None of us ever knows exactly what could have been. You can't live your life in a constant state of what-if. Believe me. I've wasted enough hours with those two little words haunting me. And it's never once brought me any peace or comfort."

"Same here." Taylor's hand settled on her stomach, and her eyes look far off for a moment. "All we can do is make the best choices we can now, because we can't go back in time."

A tear slid down Georgia's cheek. "But sometimes, we don't have choices. Life makes them for us."

"True." Caroline rubbed her thumb along the rim of her mug. "But we still can choose how we react to those kinds of situations."

They all sat in silence for a few moments, sipping on their coffee, each lost in her own thoughts. Finally, Taylor cleared her throat. "Sorry, G. We got off track a bit there. What was your SOS all about?"

Right. "Um, well, I actually need to leave town tomorrow. My boss called and the job interview for the promotion is in two days instead of next week."

"But what about the festival?" Caroline asked.

Georgia scratched behind her ear. "That's why I called you. I need your help pulling it off from afar." She pulled a binder from her briefcase and set it on the table, patting its cover. "All of the information is in here. All the vendors are arranged and know where to be and when. I've got volunteers coming Thursday and Friday to help set up, so I just need one or both of you here to direct traffic and answer questions."

Her friends both frowned at her and exchanged yet another look.

Sitting back in her chair, Georgia chewed the inside of her cheek. "If you aren't free to help, I can find someone else."

"It's not that," Caroline said. "It's just...are you sure about this?"

"I don't have a choice. I didn't set the interview time. I need to be there."

"There's always a choice." Standing, Taylor walked to the coffeepot and warmed up Georgia's and Caroline's mugs, leaving her own empty. "This is literally a chance for you to do what we just talked about—make a choice you won't regret."

"What do you want me to do? If I don't go for this promotion, then I *will* regret that." Because what else did she honestly have back in New York except for work?

Mimi's words from last week drifted back to her mind. *"Are you happy there, dear?"*

Was she? Did happiness really matter? She'd given up her chance of happiness with Nate, but what if God was giving her another chance?

Or maybe this wasn't about Nate at all. Maybe it was about Georgia. About finding happiness—joy—with or without a man.

Becoming something more than what she could define for herself.

More than what she could even *do* for herself.

"And what about leaving now? Would you regret that?" Taylor leaned back against the counter. "If you leave again right now—if you break the promises you made—who's to say you won't be sitting here in another thirteen years saying the same thing about *what-if*s that you're saying now?"

Groaning, Georgia buried her head in her hands. "You're right. You're so right. But which choice is right? How do I know?"

"What if you didn't have to make a choice at all?" Taylor said, her voice edged in challenge.

Georgia's head popped up. "What? How?"

"Don't ask me. You're the smarty with an MBA."

That made Georgia choke out a laugh. "Doesn't mean I have life smarts. Clearly."

"But God does. Pray about it," Caroline said, her voice oh so gentle. "If you want to go, we will help you with the festival stuff. But if you want to stay…we will find a way to help you do that too. Because that's what friends are for. And no matter how far you run, Georgia, you're never getting rid of us."

She didn't deserve these friends. "I don't know what to do."

"But you *do* know who you want to be." Taylor's voice was much louder than Caroline's, but just as gentle.

Yes, I do.

The whisper came deep in her soul—sure and strong, just like the table she sat at. She'd been scarred, made so many mistakes, but she didn't have to keep making more. She didn't have to let others dictate her life choices. Didn't have to let fear tell her who she was going to be.

And the person she wanted to be was one who kept her promises. Who didn't run away from her emotions. Who didn't let down the people she cared about.

Georgia might not know what was going to happen tomorrow, or next week, but she did know one thing. "I think I'm… I'm going to stay. Help with the festival, like I committed to doing."

Caroline smiled. "And what about the interview?"

"I don't know. Maybe I can ask my boss about conducting it virtually. He won't like it—and it'll probably hurt my chances of getting the job. But if I'm supposed to get the promotion, I will, right?"

It was a risk, for sure. But some things were worth taking risks for.

And keeping her promises to the town—to Nate—was one of those things.

Life had had a way of smacking him in the face lately, but at least one thing was going right.

Nate placed the hard hat Christian offered him on his head and turned a circle in the youth center. "This looks incredible."

Dust flew from the far corner where several workers were listening to a radio and cleaning the concrete in preparation to apply an epoxy floor coating, which would hopefully stand the test of time despite the many sneakers that would run across it in years to come. It was only a little before lunch, but Christian's thick work jeans were already covered in a finely coated layer of dust. "It's coming along nicely despite all the rain. Thankfully, we got the siding finished before that started up." He pointed to the walls, which looked newly finished. "And all the walls are finally done. The basic plumbing and electrical too, though the rest still needs finishing."

"So it'll definitely be completed by spring, yes?"

"For sure. The guys have been working hard. May have something to do with the extra vacation time I promised them if they put in a few extra hours this week. Pastor Jim's been begging me to help out with the church, so I've diverted a few guys that way. Didn't put us behind here at all, though."

"Smart." Hands behind his back, Nate walked a little ways in, his boots crunching fine particles of construction material. "You're so good at managing all the details."

"It's literally my job." Christian crossed his arms over his big chest and cocked an eyebrow at Nate. "Everything okay?

You seem kind of… I don't know. Down. I figured you'd be overjoyed at our progress."

"I am, man. It's great."

"Is it? Because the way you just said that is how I imagine you'd say something matter of fact, like 'I just had a dental appointment and no cavities.'"

"No cavities is always a good thing."

"But it's nothing to get overly excited about." Christian pushed on Nate's shoulder, drawing a slight chuckle from him. "And that's my point. Your dream is literally coming true. Well, Stephanie's dream, but I see how much you like the idea too. How excited it makes you. So why do you still look like you're worried the other shoe will drop? Do you not trust me and my crew—which is soon to be your crew, might I remind you?"

"You definitely do *not* have to remind me." Because how could he forget?

Christian sighed. "Just because your dad wants you to take over doesn't mean you have to."

"This again? I told you—"

"I know, but hear me out." The guys in the corner turned up their music, and Christian waved Nate into his office. They ducked inside and Christian shut the door behind them, slinging off his hard hat. His cousin's hair was pulled back in a man bun at the base of his neck. "You've invested the last few years of your life trying to get this place up and running. And from what I understand, with Georgia's help, you've finally got a business plan you think will pass muster at the council meeting this week, right?"

"Yeah." Nate hung his own hat on one of the wall pegs.

"But there's something you haven't considered. Or maybe you have, but I haven't heard you talk about it." Christian sat in the chair behind his desk, which was scattered with papers and a few coffee thermoses. The chair squeaked under his weight.

"And what's that?"

"What happens once the building is built, and the funds are there? Who is going to be leading the center?"

"We'll have to conduct interviews, find the perfect candidate."

"Why not you?"

Something thrummed in Nate's chest. He turned to face the grimy window in Christian's office. Outside, the wind blew through the trees between the center and the sidewalk. "The director position is full-time. I already have a job lined up."

"That doesn't mean anything. Not if you would rather work at the center. Seems to me this would be a great way to see things through to fruition."

The idea settled inside Nate's chest. Made a nest there, and warmed him. But no. He shook his head, turned back to face his cousin. "I can't tell Dad no. He's ready to retire. It would be selfish of me to—"

"Nate, you've never been selfish a day in your life."

"Tell that to Gramps."

"Gramps?" Christian steepled his fingers and leaned forward with his elbows on the desk. "You mean because of that time you didn't go fishing with him?"

"And then you became his favorite after."

"No, I didn't. He and I both just liked fishing."

"He treated me differently after that. I hurt him and that was selfish."

"First of all, you were a kid." Christian got up, moved around his desk, and leaned against the edge. He put his hand on Nate's shoulder and squeezed. "Second, if Gramps did take it personally, that was his problem. You were and are allowed to like different things. You don't always have to do the things others want you to do."

"I know."

"Do you?" Christian shook his head. "Man, pursuing what you love should never be cause for losing the respect or love of others. And if it is, then it wasn't really love or respect in the first place. I'm sure Gramps was just dealing with his own stuff, and it had nothing to do with you, Nate. You can't let others' expectations dictate your life choices. If you'd rather be the youth center director than CEO of Griggs Construction…do it."

"I appreciate it, man." Nate cleared his throat, looked away. "But all of this might be a moot point. The festival might fail after all, and then we won't *have* the required funds for the youth center."

"I'm confused. Didn't Georgia take over? Admittedly, I haven't interacted with her much since she got back, but that woman seems to know what she's doing."

"She does. But she's leaving. Her job interview back in New York got moved and…"

"Ah," his cousin said. "So *that's* why you're in a sour mood."

"Kind of a big deal."

"No, I get it. The woman you love is leav—"

"Dude. I *don't* love her. I did. But not anymore."

"Sure, sure." Christian waved his hand through the air like he was swatting away Nate's words. As if the very notion was ridiculous.

"I don't."

His cousin stood to his full height. "So you're telling me that no part of you wishes she was staying for other reasons? Not even for Cassie?"

Ah, Cassie. After decorating last night, she'd been so content, so sweet, snuggling under a blanket between Georgia and Nate while they'd watched *How the Grinch Stole Christmas*. She'd prattled on about how she and Georgia had to make some Christmas cookies sometime, and how she'd decorate them with pink even though it wasn't a Christmas-y color, but it was her favorite. Georgia had hugged Cass tight to herself, a look of sorrow on her face—probably because she knew what Cassie didn't. That she was leaving, and didn't know when she'd be coming back.

"Of course, Cassie will miss her," he finally said. "They've gotten close."

"And what about you? Have you gotten close?" Instead of the teasing Nate anticipated from his cousin, his question sounded sincere.

"We're just friends, and I can't entertain the notion of more. She's not staying, and I can't go. It's the same situation we found ourselves in thirteen years ago. At least this time, I know better."

"Maybe—"

But a vibration in Nate's back pocket interrupted whatever Christian was going to say. Nate pulled out his phone to find a text. The sight of Georgia's name on his screen sent a buzzing through his fingertips. "Sorry, it's from her."

"What'd she say?" Christian walked toward him.

"Since when did you get so nosy?" Nate asked, holding his phone away from his cousin's prying eyes. His own read her message—and his heart stopped.

Christian laughed. "Your eyes are bugging out like a cartoon character's so now I really have to know what she said."

Ignoring his teasing, Nate blinked at the message and read it again.

Georgia: Soooo...after much thought and deliberation, I've decided to do a virtual interview and stay on for the festival as originally planned. Hoping to stay through Christmas too. I'm sorry for all the back and forth. I hope I didn't cause you too much worry.

"Well?" Christian asked again.

"She's...staying."

"Like, for good?"

"No." Though the idea zipped through Nate and added to his nest of warmth. He shoved the thought aside. "For the festival."

"Did she say why?"

"Does it matter? The good news is she can be here and help make sure it's a success." And that's what he needed to focus on. Not on the fact that he'd get to spend more time with her. More time hearing her laugh, seeing her smile, just being near her...

"Nate."

He shoved his phone back into his pocket. "What?"

"It *does* matter. Because she stayed when she could have left—and I think you should find out why."

Chapter Nine

A woman could only stay sequestered inside for so long before her body begged for fresh air.

Georgia leaned forward on Mimi's couch and reached for her tennis shoes. From the kitchen, Mimi's warbling voice sang "How Great Thou Art" while the kitchen sink ran. Probably washing the dishes she'd used in making Georgia lunch. The irony—Georgia had come here to wait on Mimi, and the tables had been turned.

Not that Georgia wasn't helping Mimi. After all, taking over the festival had begun as such.

Now, though? It was about so much more than that. And while Georgia was grateful to be staying—to have spent the last twenty-four hours since her talk with Taylor and Caroline putting last-minute touches on her plans—she couldn't help the ache in her chest, the built-up tension in her limbs, the repeating memory of Taylor insisting she be honest with herself.

Work had always been her solace in the past, but even it couldn't drown out the emotions—the confusion—Georgia had tried so hard to hide.

Because she also couldn't stop thinking about Nate and how he'd barely replied to her declaration that she was staying for the festival. The only response he'd sent was, Great.

Thanks for letting me know. As if she'd merely informed him that apples were on sale at the market instead of telling him—showing him—she was determined to be different than Past Georgia.

No matter, though. She hadn't done it for his approval. She'd done it for her own, so she could look herself in the mirror without feeling ashamed.

Though it wouldn't have hurt if he'd shown just a little bit of happiness over her decision...

Georgia pulled on first one shoe, then the other, and stood, heading for the kitchen. She stuck her head inside and sure enough, Mimi stood at the sink with a soapy plate in hand. "I'm going for a walk, Mimi."

The singing stopped, and her grandma glanced over one shoulder. "Everything all right?"

Georgia nodded. "Just need to clear my head."

"Did you ever get ahold of your boss?"

"Yes, he finally stepped away from his meetings this morning and called me back."

Mimi set the dish on the drying rack and the towel on the counter, turning to face Georgia. "And?"

"And he's not happy, as I suspected he wouldn't be. He spent five minutes trying to convince me I was foolish for giving up this opportunity to meet with the hiring committee in person. Said it would look bad, especially with Cathy in the wings just waiting to charm them." Georgia sighed. "Maybe I *am* foolish, but I know this is the right thing."

"You're not a fool, dear. You're wise to put people and promises above your own desires." She tilted her head. "If a promotion *is* still your desire?"

"Of course it is. This doesn't change that. And Bob finally saw my point of view. At the very least, he granted my request for a virtual interview tomorrow."

"Well, that's wonderful. Now, be sure to take a coat on your walk. It's nippy out there."

That made Georgia smile. How many times had Mimi said that exact thing over the years? She'd been such a steadfast presence in Georgia's life, and Georgia had taken it for granted. But no more. "I will." She strode forward and plopped a kiss on Mimi's weathered cheek. "Love you."

Her grandmother smiled. "Love you too."

Leaving Mimi behind to continue warbling and cleaning, Georgia grabbed her coat off the rack in the living room foyer, put it on along with a pair of gloves, and stuffed her phone in her pocket. Then she opened the front door—and found Nate standing there, his hand raised as if to knock.

He took a step back. "Hi, Georgia." Some dead leaves skittered on the breeze past his feet.

How was it possible for him to get more handsome every time she saw him?

Georgia's hands made fists at her sides. "Hi, yourself." She wanted to laugh at the sudden jittery feeling in her bones, because this was Nate. How many times had he picked her up on this very stoop for a date? And yet, this felt new. Like something…more.

Which was silly.

Or was it? Because the way he was looking at her, with a subtle longing in his eyes, even a bit of apprehension…

She shifted from one foot to another. "What are you doing here?"

"Um." He blinked, then seemed to take in her state of dress. "I'm so sorry. You're going out."

"Just on a walk. Needed to get some fresh air."

He cocked his head. "Anywhere in particular?"

"No. Why?"

He waited a beat, then said, "Want to go to the bridge?"

Memories assaulted her. So many memories, good and bad. The bridge was where Nate had first asked her out. Where he'd first kissed her.

Where he'd broken her heart.

She had no real desire to go there again. But maybe that was exactly what was needed in order for them to move forward. To heal.

To be honest.

"Sure."

Without a word, she shut the door behind them and followed him to his truck. The drive only took five minutes, and soon they'd left the town behind and emerged into a wooded world of serenity. Birds chirped, the breeze blew light and cold against her cheeks, and Pineberry Creek rustled along the dirt path as they walked toward the natural travertine bridge. Today there was no one else hiking the trail, and it felt as if they'd entered their own world.

Then again, it always had felt that way with Nate.

Georgia exhaled a breath and shook out her hands as they made their way around a bend and finally saw the bridge there in all its glory, nearly two hundred feet high and arcing over a cave-like tunnel that was about four hundred feet in length. Piles of large lava rocks and boulders spread throughout the tunnel, all surrounding a pool of water that originated on the other side.

The steady flow of the distant waterfall created peaceful white noise as Nate started to climb, glancing back to make sure Georgia kept pace with him. Her leg muscles burned, but it was a good burn, and soon they'd traversed to the middle of the tunnel, where their favorite large flat rock overlooked the water below. Nate helped pull Georgia up the last high step until they stood toe to toe on the top.

"Thanks," she said, her voice suddenly hoarse.

His gaze caressed her features, and he visibly swallowed. "It's been a long time since I've come here. Not since that night…"

"Really?"

"Really."

"Huh." Her heart tap dancing against her chest, Georgia pulled her gaze from his and sat on the edge of the rock where a patch of light warmed its surface. Her legs dangled over the side.

"What does that mean? *Huh*?" Nate lowered himself beside her, leaving only an inch between them.

Georgia played with the zipper on her jacket. "Just that I would have figured you and Stephanie…"

"Georgia, this was *our* place. Stephanie and I…" He hmm'd. "It's harder to talk about than I thought it'd be."

"You don't have to—"

"Yes, I do." A pause. "I want to." He waited a moment, staring at his lap. Then, "I'm guessing it was a shock to hear that Stephanie and I got married so soon after you left."

The prideful part of her wanted to say it hadn't bothered her at all. But she'd promised to be honest, at least with herself, and she wanted to be honest with him too. If she was ever going to be able to move forward, to move on, she needed to do this. Besides, he was her friend, and if a person couldn't be truthful with their friends…

"It broke me, Nate."

"What?" His head swiveled and he looked down at her, brow furrowed, eyes searching. "I guess I figured you left and never looked back."

"I tried, but as you said, our bond was so strong. I was miserable in New York without you." She sighed and looked out across the tunnel, at the rocks scattered like every memory from their past. "I even…" Did she need to go there?

Nate leaned closer, and their shoulders touched. "You even...what?"

"I was going to come home that spring, to see you. To see if we could work things out somehow." Biting the inside of her cheek, Georgia tasted the tiniest hint of blood. "But it was too late. *I* was too late. You and Stephanie had already fallen in love."

"Peach..." He breathed her nickname out like a prayer, like a curse.

"I know. But I don't begrudge you your happiness. Maybe I did, once. But now I know Cassie, and she would never have existed if you and Stephanie hadn't found each other." A tear dripped down her cheek. "And I'm so sorry for all the pain you've experienced. So sorry for all the heartache I caused you. For a long time, I hated you for giving me up so easily when I couldn't seem to get you out of my head, my heart, my every thought." More tears came, and she swiped them away, unable to look at him even though she felt his gaze warm on her. "But now, I'm glad that you and Stephanie had each other. That you loved and were loved even though I'd abandoned you."

And oh, she hated how her chin trembled, but she was done hiding her emotions. Maybe love *was* a distraction, but keeping it bottled up inside was not any better.

"Hey." Nate's hand gently met Georgia's cheek, and he turned it until she faced him. His thumb wiped away her tears and then pressed against the cleft of her chin. "Thank you for telling me all of that. I know it couldn't have been easy."

"No, but it was time you knew the truth. All of it."

His hand slid down, back into his lap, and he frowned, exhaling. "Then I owe you the truth as well."

"What do you mean?"

"You'll probably think worse of me when you hear."

She leaned her head against his shoulder, breathed in his masculine scent of clean soap and pine. "That's not possible. You're the best man I know."

He laughed, but there was something terse in it. Whatever he had to say clearly troubled him. It took him several long moments before he began. "Stephanie and I had known each other our whole lives. She was always the girl my parents..."

"It's okay, Nate. I know your mom was never my biggest fan. And that Stephanie was the golden girl." Of course she was—she was the pastor's daughter. But she was also kind, and good, and if Nate had fallen for anyone, Georgia was glad it had been her.

Sighing, he set his head against Georgia's. "When you left, I was pretty broken up. Stephanie was also really upset the rest of that summer. I don't know if you remember Finn Jacobs, but she'd apparently had a huge crush on him for years and he'd been a jerk to her. Anyway, we basically bonded over the fact that we were both heartbroken. Started hanging out all the time. She made me smile, made me laugh, but I never...that is, she wasn't you, Peach."

A shiver ran up Georgia's spine.

"And that's not to say I didn't love her. I did. It was just... different. It wasn't fiery and passionate and exciting like our love was. It was quiet, and steady, and good—kind of like Stephanie. We started as friends, but then we grew closer..." His breath shuddered in and out.

Georgia grabbed his hand, and he threaded his fingers through hers. Facing the truth of the past—together. "It's okay. Whatever you want to tell me, it's okay."

It took him a while, but finally he spoke again. "She ended up pregnant."

Georgia sucked in a breath.

"We got married right away, and nobody ever knew the

real reason. They all just assumed we'd fallen head over heels in love. And we let them."

Oh, wow. Georgia let Nate's confession sink in. He hadn't forgotten her. Had been just as gutted as she was. But instead of isolating himself like she had, he'd sought comfort in someone else.

"Thank you for telling me that."

"You deserved to know."

They sat there in silence, absorbing the impact of the honesty they'd both given. But a question niggled. "She was pregnant? But Cassie…"

"Is only seven. Right. Stephanie miscarried that first baby."

"I'm so sorry."

"I blamed myself for a long time. Like it was God's punishment. But through a lot of prayer and processing the grief with Stephanie, we both came to the conclusion that God doesn't work like that. He wants to give us good things, and we decided that no matter how quickly our marriage came to be—and even if we *were* misguided in getting married for the reasons we did—that we'd committed to our marriage and were serious about our vows. So we got to know each other better, deepened our friendship, did what we could to be the best husband and wife we knew how to be…and then there was Cassie." His voice softened with each word. "And Cassie is the best thing God's *ever* given me."

Georgia squeezed his hand. "She is more than a good gift. I love that she is the product of so much grief and pain. That something good came out of it all."

"I'm discovering *that's* how God works." Nate pulled away, turned to her. "He's really good at giving second chances."

Georgia allowed her gaze to meet his once more. Her

mouth went dry. Because his eyes were so blue but warm too—ardent and filled with something she couldn't define. "Nate..."

"You stayed, Georgia."

She blinked. "What?"

"You could have run home to New York instead of staying to help with the festival. But you didn't."

"No. I didn't."

He studied her for a moment before lifting his free hand and trailing his fingertip down the curves of her cheek. "Why?"

The question, along with his feather-soft touch, broke something open inside of her. "Because I didn't like who I'd become. And if I'm honest—" she licked her lips "—I wasn't ready to leave."

"I'm not ready for you to leave either." Nate's face came closer, so near their foreheads touched. Then their noses.

Georgia couldn't make herself pull away. Not in this moment, when his breath mingled with hers, or in the next, when she shut her eyes and let him, at long last, kiss her.

Their lips pressed together, and nothing else mattered.

She angled toward him and wound her arms around his neck, and his arms slipped around her waist—holding her safe, like she was the most precious thing in the world.

And when he pulled away, it took a dizzying moment before reality crashed back in. "Nate."

He pushed a stray hair behind her ear and smiled softly. "I know. You're still leaving after Christmas. But I'm not sorry it happened. I'll always care for you, Georgia, whether you're near or far."

Oh, her heart. She could no longer deny that she wanted him—wanted this.

But she wanted the promotion too. Had worked hard for

it. Had slaved away for years, building a life. She couldn't throw it all away for a mere chance at happiness. For the possibly misguided hope that someone would finally choose her, and wouldn't leave…

Could she?

If only there was a way to have it all.

But life didn't work that way.

Still, what else could she say? Leaning forward, Georgia kissed him softly once more. "I'm not sorry either. And I feel the same way."

He shouldn't have kissed Georgia yesterday.

His heart had already been scraped raw by her disappearance and reappearance, and then the threat of her disappearance again—but there he'd gone giving in to the impulse of so many years of pent-up emotion and longing. Of wondering…what if?

Now he knew *what if.*

If he'd only kept Stephanie as a friend…

If he'd remained true to Georgia, to his principles…

But he also couldn't bring himself to regret his past actions, because he couldn't imagine a world without Cassie in it. God truly had redeemed the past. And then he'd brought Georgia back into Nate's life.

The only problem? She was soon to leave it. And he'd kissed her.

Not that he regretted that either. He'd said as much, and he'd meant it. He couldn't let their conversation pass without showing her how he felt, even if it changed nothing between them.

Even if it had made it impossible to focus on anything else since then…not even the town council meeting he was currently sitting through.

Currently running.

"What was that, Mrs. Brightley?" The fluorescent lights of the Pineberry School's multipurpose room seemed brighter than usual tonight, though Nate could still see the rows of chairs spread out before him where he stood on the small stage behind a podium. His fellow townspeople's dedication to the goings on of Pineberry had always amazed him, but never more so than eight days before Christmas.

The plump woman standing at the microphone between the chair rows fisted her hip and harrumphed. "I said, when are we going to talk more about my roosters?"

Seriously?

Nate threw on a tight smile. "As I've said before, your particular neighborhood has an HOA and they—"

"Mr. Walker has assured me he can change that. I can't wait for *him* to be mayor."

If it wasn't for the smug look on Wayne Walker's face—the way he straightened his shoulders from his front-row seat and grinned as big as an elephant—Nate would offer his agreement on the subject. Not that he hadn't enjoyed parts of his job. Of course he had.

It had allowed him to get to this point…to this moment right here.

He cleared his throat. "Thank you for your thoughts on the subject, Sally. Now, if there aren't any more orders of business?" Nate's gaze skimmed the room—bumping over Christian, Cassie, and his parents in the front row, and nearly stopping on Elizabeth Eaton and Frances…and mostly, Georgia…on the opposite side—but nobody raised their hand. "Good. Then I'd like to propose the finalization of the Pineberry Youth Center's business plan."

If possible, Wayne Walker's shoulders got even straighter.

He turned and whispered something in the ear of town council member and the owner of Ponderosa Market, Rupert Kelley.

The other three members of the town council waited quietly on the other side of Mr. Kelley while Nate continued. "I want to first say thank you to our esteemed council, as their feedback has given me the impetus I needed to examine the sustainability of the project."

Wayne preened and very well may have strutted around the room if he hadn't been sitting.

Nate caught Georgia's gaze. She smiled at him and rolled her eyes.

He had to hold back a grin. "With the help of someone who has extensive business knowledge, I've revamped our business plan, which you'll be getting a copy of from a very cute helper." Nate winked at Cassie, who hopped up and took a stack of papers from Dad's hands. Together they spread out and handed the papers down the aisles. Older ladies cooed at Cassie, who grinned in her pigtails and the red sparkly tutu she'd insisted on wearing for the occasion.

The whirring heater kicked on somewhere overhead, and Nate allowed everyone a few moments to look the plan over before continuing. "As you can see, we've made several small tweaks throughout, but allow me to draw your attention to page three." Paper rustled as people turned pages, and the five town council members looked not at him but intently at the papers in their hands. "Here we've detailed two very important additions to the plan—two things that will ensure sustainability and consistency in the guidance and direction of the youth center."

Murmuring and nodding joined the white noise buzzing in the room. "The first is a qualified director. This person will be responsible for overseeing the center as a whole—from the hiring of employees to the creation and managing of programs. Hiring the right person is crucial to the center's continued success from year to year."

Christian's words from a few nights ago echoed in Nate's mind: *"Why not you?"*

He shoved them away, eyes flitting inexplicably to Georgia. Her nose scrunched at his sudden scrutiny, but she nodded—an encouragement to keep going. That he was doing well.

That this was almost done. All the hard work, all the time spent…it would be worth it in the end.

"Finally, we've incorporated the strategy of securing grants to help aid in keeping the center afloat so we don't have to keep relying year after year solely on funds from festivals and the town coffers."

Wayne frowned, bringing the paper closer to his face.

"Are there any questions?"

Each of the town council members and a few townspeople asked for clarifications, but since they'd already seen a previous version of the business plan, the questions were light and addressing them easy. Georgia had prepared him for this, and it went as smoothly as it could.

Even Wayne Walker didn't have a negative word to say about it. In fact, he said nothing at all, just sat there pouting and growing red in the face, like a grizzly forced into restraints.

In the end, the council approved his plan, and before Nate knew it, he was off the stage and pulling Cassie up into a hug. "You were so good, Daddy."

"Thanks, pumpkin. I couldn't have done it without my helper."

"You mean Georgia?"

His mother grunted and stepped up beside them. "Come

on, Cassie. It's nearly bedtime, and your father has his constituents to speak with."

Cassie started to protest, but Nate gave her a look. Slipping from his arms to the ground, Cassie followed her grandparents out the back door. He heard her exclaim about something and rush out. Before he could ask her why she'd shouted, Nate was joined by Jason Anderson and a few others who patted him on the back and said how much they looked forward to helping out at the youth center.

"Really great job, man." Jason clapped him on the back and turned to Christian, who was talking to Caroline and Taylor. Nate heard mention of pizza, and his cousin gave him a head nod before the four of them headed out.

"You did do a really great job, you know," the voice he'd been waiting to hear all night said from behind him.

With a grin, he turned to find Georgia there, pulling on her coat and scarf, her blond hair in waves around her shoulders. "Thanks. I'm glad it passed. One big day down, one more to go."

"*One* more?" She laughed. "You really haven't planned many events, have you, Mr. Mayor?"

"I thought that was obvious from the get-go."

"True." Her lips tilted into a grin. All around them, the crowd thinned as people left to make dinner or prepare for work and the last few days of school before winter break began. "For your information, the festival will be a three-day event, because tomorrow is when I start setting everything up. Then Friday the rest will be done, and Saturday is the actual festival, of course. And now that my interview is over, I can focus fully on the event."

"I meant to text and ask how it went but got busy prepping the meeting materials. So?"

She bit her lip. "The interview went as well as can be expected. I'm hoping my work speaks for itself."

"I'm sure it will. If you were half as brilliant as you were when fixing up my business plan, you've got the job in the bag."

"Thank you."

"I mean it, Georgia. You're talented and smart and…" Blinking, he turned toward the podium. "Here, let me gather up my stuff, and I'll walk you home."

"Okay."

While he headed up onto the stage and unplugged his laptop, rolled up cords, and packed it all away into his messenger bag, she walked the now empty aisles and gathered up papers that had been left behind by meeting goers. The heels of her boots clicked on the rubber flooring.

When they were both done with their tasks, Georgia met Nate at the bottom of the stage steps, handing him the proposals. "Here."

"Thanks. And thanks again for all of your help on this. I really couldn't have done it without you."

"Your presentation was great. I think they really loved the changes we made—especially the part about the director." She studied him, her lips pressed together. "Have you considered…"

Nate stuffed the papers into his bag. "What?"

"It's just, the director needs to be passionate about the center. He or she needs to love people, kids especially, and have a sense of what this town in particular needs. If anyone's qualified to do it, it's you."

"Have you been talking to my cousin?"

"No, I haven't really seen him since I've been back. But if he agrees with me, then he's as smart as I remember." She winked, and he laughed.

"I'll tell him you say so."

"Truth be told, I already have a job lined up—taking over as CEO for my dad's company. But if that wasn't waiting for me, I actually would love to be director. As soon as Christian suggested it, I got all kinds of ideas."

"So talk with your dad about it."

"It's not that easy."

"Actually, it is." She put her hand on his arm. "Nate, in ten years, you could be a decade into a job you hate or one you love. The choice is yours."

"People are depending on me."

"You're not the only one who can take over for your dad. He's a reasonable man. Talk with him."

"Maybe." He glanced away, brow furrowed. Took a breath. "You ready to go?"

"Sure, if we're all done here."

"Yep." The chairs remained out, but the school custodian would stack and move them into position in the morning. There wasn't anything else he needed to do now except go home and relish his victory.

But he didn't want to be alone. This was their victory, after all.

"Hey." His gaze found hers again. "Want to grab a bite to eat? Celebrate?"

Georgia's hand left his arm, and her features twisted into a pained expression. "I'm not sure that's a good idea."

Oh. Right. "Yeah, sure, of course. I—"

"There's just a lot to do the next few days, for the festival and all that."

Was she just making excuses, or was she really that busy with festival prep? Maybe it didn't matter. Because regardless of whether she got the promotion, Georgia *was* leaving in a week or so. Maybe sooner.

They'd cleared the air between them, she'd helped him out, and they were friends. That was all that there was to it.

And even if *he* couldn't get the kiss out of his brain, that didn't mean the same was true for her. Either way, it was probably smarter to avoid being alone together more than necessary.

It would only cause more confusion. More trouble.

And his growing feelings for Georgia Carrington were already troublesome enough.

"Sure. I understand." Nate flicked off the lights, and momentarily they were alone in the dark together. He could make out the outline of her face against the streaks of light coming through the cracks around the doorway that led to the school's parking lot. And was it his imagination, or did she lean close, close, closer to him?

But then she stopped, pivoted, and flung open the door to leave—and he bumped into her where she halted in the doorway, just staring at what lay before them.

A frosting of white, with more coming down.

She stepped outside, holding her hand palm up and outstretched. "Nate, look."

Snow dotted her hair, and the light from the parking lot streetlamps framed her in a soft glow. "It's beautiful."

But his compliment—which had slipped out—didn't seem to please her. Instead, she turned to him, near panic in her eyes. "It's snowing. Snowing, Nate."

Oh no. "The festival."

"It's got to stop soon, right? Snowstorms can't just come out of nowhere like this. Well, they can, and we knew there was a chance of one, but it was only like ten percent and there were no other signs…" She started to pace, reminding Nate of himself last week after the church had flooded.

But he was not calm like Georgia had been. He understood the panic inside.

Because if the snow didn't let up—if it kept going as hard as it was coming down right now—there'd be no way to access Malcolm's property in three days' time.

Which meant that all of their hard work, all the victories they'd just had, wouldn't matter.

No festival meant no money for the budget…which meant no youth center at all.

Chapter Ten

The snow had finally let up.

But it might be too little, too late.

"Is the festival really gonna be canceled?" Cassie—whose last day of school before break had been officially proclaimed a snow day—looked at Georgia with big eyes. She appeared so small and vulnerable sitting at Mimi's kitchen table in her play clothes, her hair in a braid down her back, waiting for Georgia to make a last-minute breakfast for them all while Nate tried for the hundredth time to get ahold of someone who might be willing to plow the road up to Malcolm's farm.

"We're doing our best so that doesn't happen, sweetie." Georgia flipped a pancake at the stove and looked desperately toward Mimi sitting beside Cassie, drinking her coffee. She'd graciously agreed to watch Nate's daughter today while Georgia and Nate attempted to work on a solution for the festival. "We got some stuff set up yesterday before the second part of the storm blew in and completely blocked the road—the North Pole in the barn, the indoor food stations, that sort of thing."

But after the snow that got dumped again last night, the road was impassable until either the snow melted—which wasn't likely given the expected low temps for tomorrow—or a plow could be hired. Thankfully Main Street had been plowed, and the highways would be fine, so out-of-town guests wouldn't have a problem getting through.

But if they couldn't get up to the farm, then the festival was doomed.

"But how are we gonna—"

"My dear." Mimi patted the girl's arm. "Your daddy and Georgia are working out all the details. And besides all that, God's on the job. Don't you worry. It will all work out exactly as it should."

The smell of syrup and pancake batter permeated the warm kitchen. Georgia would find it cozy here, tucked away with all the people she loved best while the window outside showcased the winter's splendor—except for what it meant for the festival.

What it meant for Nate.

She could hear the low rumble of his voice from the living room, where she could picture him pacing in front of the fireplace mantel. It mingled with the bright chatter of Mimi and Cassie, who had moved on to talking about the kind of snowman the girl wanted to build today.

Georgia finished up her current batch of pancakes and slipped them onto the table. Then she kissed the top of Mimi's head, gave Cassie's braid a playful tug, and moved into the living room, where Nate sat forward on the couch cushion, staring at the phone in his hand.

He glanced up at Georgia as she entered.

"Anything?" she asked.

"No."

Frowning, she walked to the mantel and adjusted Mimi's stocking, which was slightly askew. "How can there not be any snowplows available?"

"The storm came on so suddenly, and several operators are off work for the holidays. There aren't that many up in this area to begin with. Because of the upcoming weekend, the ones that are available are needed to clear roads for holiday travel."

Georgia whirled, hands on her hips. "I still don't understand why the ones that came through Main Street this morning couldn't have made a slight deviation up the road toward Malcolm's."

"They're contracted with the town, but only for Main Street, Hardscrabble, and Anasazi Way. They said the steeper roads are slower going and take more passes, and they're on a tight schedule as it is." Nate released a groan. He looked so tired, so worn, and she wanted more than anything to take this burden from him.

"So we're stuck? There's no other possible solution?"

"Well."

Georgia's eyes narrowed on him, and she strode to the couch, lowered herself beside him. "What?"

"There's only one other thing I can think of, but it'll never work."

"Why not? If there's even an inkling of a chance it might—"

"It won't." Nate huffed out an exasperated laugh. "Not unless you can figure out a way to get Wayne Walker to loan us the personal plow he mounted on his truck."

She blinked. "You're saying the future mayor has a plow?"

"Yeah, he built it a few years ago because he was tired of hiring someone to come out every time it snowed. You remember how his bed-and-breakfast is kind of off the beaten path? One main building but it's also got several cabins against the mountainside."

"Sure, I remember." The Walker B&B had been situated at the north end of town for who knew how many years or generations—certainly since Georgia had lived there. "And he never loans it out?"

"Oh, sure he does." Nate fixed her with a look. "To people and causes he likes."

Ah. "I see." Standing, Georgia marched toward the front door and took her jacket off the hook.

"What are you doing?" Nate asked, getting up from the couch.

Smiling at him, she threw on her coat and gloves. "I'm going to go see a man about a plow."

"Georgia—"

"Nate, everyone has something they want. I just have to figure out what Wayne is willing to trade for that."

He stood there staring at her, shaking his head. "You're amazing, you know that?"

His words twined through her, bandaging the places inside where she'd been wounded in the past. "I'm just a woman on a mission. And while there is breath in my lungs, I'm not going to sit by and let this festival fail. I know what it means to you, Nate."

Knew what the youth center meant to him—whether he ended up accepting the job as director or not. Though she really hoped he did. It was perfect for him. He was perfect for it.

And it would tie him even more to Pineberry...

But she couldn't afford to think that way, no matter how much her heart and mind wanted to linger on that moment together—that kiss—three days ago.

"Thank you, Georgia." He stepped forward and looped her scarf around her neck, his gaze skimming the features of her face, stopping briefly on her lips before flitting back up to her eyes. "Should I come with you?"

It took her a moment to speak past the dryness in her throat. "I think I can talk more sense into Wayne without you there. But why don't you spend time calling our volunteers, letting them know to be on standby today for when we get the road plowed? In the meantime, take to social media and let people know the festival is still on."

"Even though we don't know for sure it will be?"

She tipped her nose into the air. "You doubt my powers of persuasion?"

He chuckled. "I learned a long time ago to never doubt you, Georgia Peach."

"Good. You just keep up that faith, Mr. Mayor." Tossing him a wink, she strode out the door and toward her car, swinging it onto the freshly plowed road and driving toward the bed-and-breakfast, the whole way formulating a plan in her mind.

Downtown bustled with shoppers on this Friday morning. Even Caroline's shop seemed to have a decent number of cars in the lot. Georgia still needed to follow up on their conversation from Monday, where Caroline had implied the store wasn't doing so well. Maybe Georgia could offer some thoughts...

Though what could she really do? She was leaving after Christmas.

Driving past the youth center, Georgia gripped the steering wheel tighter. From the outside, it looked nearly completed—even had a door now. She hated that she wouldn't be here for the grand opening this spring. Maybe she could make a spontaneous trip out. Though if she received the promotion, work would keep her even busier than it already did.

Across the street, several Griggs Construction trucks filled the church parking lot, and workers came through the front doors carrying old carpet and materials. What would it look like inside when all was said and done?

Georgia wouldn't know—because she'd be back in New York, living the life she'd built for herself.

A hollow ache thrummed in her chest.

Breathing out, she refocused on the matter at hand. What did Wayne want? His kids had been ahead of her in school, so all she knew of the man was the arrogance he'd displayed toward Nate at the town council meeting and her few random interactions with him at community events. But as she pulled into the bed-and-breakfast—a large quaint log cabin with a wraparound porch—she remembered the most important thing.

He was a businessman in a small town, which meant his livelihood depended on others' good opinions of him.

Georgia turned off her car's ignition and made her way out of the vehicle and up the steps, passing an adorable porch swing that overlooked Main Street. She entered the front door to find a college-aged woman with a pixie cut sitting behind a computer at a carved wooden reception desk. "Welcome to Walker B&B! How can I help you today?"

"Hi, I'm Georgia Carrington. Is Mr. Walker available? I need to speak to him about an urgent business matter."

"Let me see." The woman stood and stuck her head into a doorway just behind the desk. "Grandpa? There's a Georgia Carrington here to see you."

"Thank you, Eloise. I'll be right there." A moment later, Wayne's large figure filled the doorway. He hiked up his pants and eyed Georgia with curiosity. "Well, well, Ms. Carrington. This is unexpected. Come in, come in."

Georgia smiled at Eloise and followed Wayne into an office with a window that faced a small driveway. And there, just outside, sat a large black truck with a mounted plow. Georgia's heartbeat quickened, but she schooled her features. She couldn't look too eager. This was a business meeting, not a plea for mercy. Turning, she took the measure of the man sitting behind the desk as he waved his hand toward a chair opposite him.

His cowboy hat hung on a peg behind him, and his bald head reflected the light above. "Sit, please, and tell me why you've come."

"That—" she pointed toward the plow "—is why I've come."

"My plow?" His eyebrows rose. "Interesting indeed." Folding his hands, he leaned forward on the desk. "This wouldn't have anything to do with the festival tomorrow, now would it?"

"It might." Georgia circled the chair and perched on the edge of its seat, her straight shoulders communicating that she would not cower before this man—a bully if ever she saw one. Or Nate seemed to think so, anyway. But Georgia understood him. All of her years in corporate America weren't wasted on Pineberry, after all. Georgia's lips tipped into a smile. "I was wondering how much you charge to rent it out."

He tsked. "Now, now, I don't rent Bessy there out to just anyone. Only causes I really believe in." Wayne flicked a metal ball at the end of a Newton's cradle decoration sitting on his desk. The ball swung out and back, hitting the series of balls beside it and causing the one at the other end to propel outward. "Tell me, Ms. Carrington. Why would I help out the man who has been thwarting my efforts to see a senior center constructed in our town? Especially when the very failure of your festival gets me what I want—an excuse to use the new building the way I see fit?"

And there it was. Georgia didn't flinch. "Because *you* don't want to be the town bad guy."

"And how would I be?"

"People around here know you have a plow. It might get out that you were unwilling to lend assistance." She sighed and shook her head, as if the very idea made her sad. "And how would that look, for the future mayor to not take pity on the current mayor simply because they disagreed on a few points? I'd think you'd be eager to lend your assistance to the event that so many of your future constituents have put countless hours and hopes into."

Wayne studied her with shrewd eyes under his bushy brows. His hand darted out and stopped the motion of the kinetic decoration. "Are you threatening me?" His tone was more amused than offended.

She had to laugh at that too. "Not at all. Just reminding you that everyone here knows everyone's business, and people frequent your establishment and elected you as mayor because you are respected in this town." Georgia cocked her head. "If people find out you were less than helpful—and they will, because it's Pineberry—then that might change. I'd hate to see your future tenure as mayor be less than fruitful because you lost the entire respect of the town over one minor grievance."

"Some might not call it minor. I've got a lot of residents who want that senior center."

"And just as many who want the youth center." An idea sparked so suddenly, Georgia couldn't breathe. Where had that come from? Perhaps divine inspiration had struck. She sat forward in her chair. "Mr. Walker, you might not know this about me, but my background is in business planning and finance. What if I could figure out a way to use my experience to get you and Nate what you both want?"

"I'm intrigued. What are you suggesting?"

"You want a senior adults center. Nate wants a youth center. Why not combine the two into one big community center, with programs for both? Honestly, what you really need is a parks and recreation department that could oversee such a thing, as well as add other programs like sports leagues, summer camps, etcetera. That department could also oversee the finances and ensure grants are coming in to finance at least the youth portion of the center, if not the whole thing."

"You make some extremely interesting points." Wayne sat back in his chair and set his hands over his stomach, his fingers tapping in succession. "All right, I'll loan you the plow on one condition."

"Don't worry, we will take good care of it."

"That goes without saying. But what I want is for you to create a business plan for what you're proposing—the joint community center. The parks and recreation department. All of it. And I want it on my desk next week. Before I officially take over as mayor."

That would be hours of work. And in the end, Nate might hate the idea...

But if they wanted to make the festival happen, this was the only way Georgia could see it happening.

Standing, she offered her hand across the desk. "Mr. Walker, you've got yourself a deal."

"And you've got yourself a plow."

The lane to Malcolm's farm had been cleared, the booths set up, the food trucks placed—and all was prepared for tomorrow's festival.

Once again, Georgia had come through.

Once again, she'd showcased her brilliance.

And once again, Nate had fallen for her.

The truth had hit him today as he'd watched her work, watched her tease Cassie, watched her take time to snuggle baby goats with him and his daughter when there was still so much to do.

In each of those moments, he'd tried to resist but was as powerless against the resurgence of his love for her as he'd be against real ocean swells. It had snuck up on him, drowning him with unexpected force.

And now, he couldn't breathe.

Darkness had descended around them as he sat on the stoop of Malcolm's house, draining a third mug of coffee. The night sky stretched dark and clear overhead, the moon showing off its splendor, the stars playing a supporting role with their own glittering light. The volunteers had all gone home save Georgia and Caroline, who were making dinner with Cassie's help.

Nate's rear was nearly numb with the cold, but it was better than being inside the warm kitchen with Georgia. Such a domestic setting inspired domestic thoughts—ones his tattered heart couldn't afford.

The screen door screeched open, and Nate turned to find Malcolm there, his cowboy hat low over his eyes, a mug in his hands, one of his border collies at his heels. His old friend didn't say anything, just sat beside Nate and drank his coffee while the dog—Gizmo, Nate thought—lay at both of their feet.

Finally, Malcolm spoke. "Didn't take you for a coward."

"Excuse me?"

"You're hiding. You're out here when you should be in there." Malcolm jutted his chin toward the house.

"Maybe I am hiding." Nate set his empty mug next to his right foot and tucked his hands inside his coat pocket. "But not because I'm afraid."

"No? Then why are you avoiding her?"

"Because..." He blinked. "Wait, how did you know that?" It's not like he'd told Malcolm what he was feeling for Georgia. His friend was more of the strong and silent type—generous to a fault, but not exactly chatty.

"It's fairly obvious. The way you feel about her." Malcolm

stared off into the distance, where his lavender fields waved in the light breeze of the clear night. "Have you told her yet?"

"I can't. But not because I'm a coward. It's because I can't ask her to stay."

"And you can't go." Malcolm didn't even question it. It was a fact, and they all knew it. Even if he wasn't taking over for Dad, he wouldn't rip Cassie away from the only home she'd ever known. Her family. She'd already lost too much.

"No."

"But sorry, why can't you ask her to stay?"

"She's got a life, and dreams, back in New York. She's up for a promotion, and she loves what she does. I can't stand in the way of all that."

"Hmm." Malcolm drained his mug, then stood. "Seems to me that Georgia is a really smart woman who is capable of making her own decisions—but she needs all the facts to be able to do so." He walked back inside, the door slamming with an echo into the quiet of the night.

Nate groaned, and after a few more minutes of solitude, heaved himself up and headed inside. It smelled like garlic and butter, and laughter and chatter filled the home. Caroline and Taylor were on the couch in the living room, which was decorated for Christmas with a large tree in front of the window and stockings hanging from the mantel. Malcolm's three dogs lazed in front of the fireplace, and Malcolm rocked in a large recliner, his eyes fixed sharply on Caroline, who was telling a story with a wide smile on her face and her hands flying wildly about with emotion.

A low murmur of voices emanated from the kitchen, and Nate followed them to find Cassie and Georgia there—Georgia minding something on the stove while Cassie sat on the kitchen island, legs swinging as she talked Georgia's ear off about something. Georgia responded with a glance over her shoulder and a nod, fully engaged in what Nate's daughter was saying. A pot of pasta boiled on the stovetop, and Georgia stirred something in a separate pot.

He couldn't help himself. Nate leaned against the doorway and just watched the two of them—enjoying what would probably be one of the last of such moments.

After a few moments, Cassie caught sight of him and leaped down. "Daddy! Georgia's making pa-sketti and garlic bread and it smells sooooooo good. She also made a salad, and that doesn't look too good, but that's not her fault 'cause salad's just gross."

Georgia laughed, clearly unaffected by Cassie's assessment. "It'll make you grow big and strong, so you'll eat a little bit for me, won't you?"

Cassie made a face. "I guess so." Then she smiled at Nate. "Can I go pet the goats again before dinner?"

"Maybe afterward, sweetie. I'm guessing dinner's almost ready."

"About ten minutes or so," Georgia said. She set her ladle down and turned to Cassie, placing her hands on her shoulders. "Tell you what. After we eat, if it's okay with your daddy, you can help me make sure the reindeer antlers fit the smallest goats. I got two different kinds for the Santa pictures tomorrow, and I haven't had a chance to see which ones will work."

"Ooh, can we, please, Daddy?" Cassie bounced on her toes.

"Sure, pumpkin." He ruffled her hair, and she ran off toward the living room shouting about goats.

"That girl." Georgia's eyes sparkled as she turned back to the spaghetti sauce on the stovetop. "So much more energy than I have about now."

"You've been working hard." Nate came up beside her and held out his hand. "Here, let me."

"You know how to make spaghetti sauce?"

"Looks like you've done all the hard work. Now it's just about stirring it so it doesn't stick, right?" He nudged her with a grin.

She smiled back. "Sounds so simple when you put it like that." Georgia handed over the ladle and leaned back against the counter facing Nate. She kneaded her neck with her fingertips. "Today was long, but I'm excited to see it all come together. The weather's supposed to hold and the sun come out tomorrow. I think it's going to be a lovely day."

"I still can't believe you did all of this. And that you got Wayne to loan us the plow. You never did tell me how you convinced him."

Georgia's fingers stopped. "About that."

"What?"

"The only way I could get him to agree was to give him something he wanted in exchange—a new business plan." She winced.

"For what?"

"For a joint community center—something that marries both of your ideas into one place. A space that serves the entire community, with an emphasis on seniors and the youth." She held up her hands in defense. "I know it's not ideal, and it doesn't mean the community will approve it—not when they've already approved your plans."

Brilliant woman. "Georgia."

She rushed on, as if afraid to hear what he was going to say. "And I know it doesn't meet your vision for the center, but I thought, what if you didn't have to constantly worry that he was going to undo all the hard work you put into this? What if you worked together and both got what you wanted? Since I'm the one drawing up the plans, I'll be sure to give the right emphasis to things, to ensure that the youth center portion doesn't get lost to the senior citizens portion." She peeked up at him. "Even that the job description for the director position would be ideally suited to you, if you decide to apply." Her eyes shone with hope. "I know you've said you don't want it, but..."

Nate stirred the spaghetti sauce, his brain whirring. "It's not about wanting it. It's about abandoning the plans I had. About whether what I want is actually more important than what others need me to be. That's no small thing."

"Don't you see? Your compassion and empathy are the exact things that would make you the perfect director. What you want *does* matter, Nate."

Malcolm's words from earlier swirled in his mind. Then he shook them away. "We don't always get what we want."

"We definitely don't if we never go after new opportunities."

His hand stilled and his gaze shot up to meet hers. She was talking about the director position, but could she also mean...?

But going after her would mean asking her to choose. Though like Malcolm said—she was a smart woman. Maybe he *should* tell her how he felt.

He set the ladle down. Inhaled a deep breath. Swallowed. Opened his mouth to—

"And speaking of new opportunities... I got the promotion."

If she'd kicked him in the chest, it would have hurt less. "What? When?"

"Earlier today. My boss called during all the hustle and bustle, told me they need me back the Monday after Christmas. They want to get me trained up and ready to hit the ground running the first of the year."

"Congrats." He breathed the word out in a rush and forced a smile onto his face. "That's great."

She looked down at her sweater and played with a button. "Is it?"

"Of course it is." He paused. "Isn't it? This is what you wanted. Your big break."

"No, yeah, it is." She crossed her arms over her chest. "I guess I just wondered…"

"Wondered what?"

She sighed. "Nothing. It's great. Everything is working out like it should, right? There's no reason I shouldn't be happy." Her eyes found his again. "Is there?"

How much he wanted to pull her into his arms, scream at her that she could be happy here, with him and Cassie. But he wasn't the one who dictated what made her happy, now was he? Because what if she gave up this opportunity and then regretted it? What if this little life in this little town—with him, the guy who had failed so many people before—wasn't enough for Georgia?

It hadn't been enough for her thirteen years ago. And sure, they were older, but why would now really be any different? Georgia was ambitious, and he loved that about her. He wouldn't want to hold her back.

And yeah, she *was* a smart woman, which meant she had to know how he felt about her. He didn't go around kissing just anyone or telling them his darkest secrets. And if she was still choosing to leave…then who was he to stop her?

"No." He turned back to the sauce, which was clumping at the bottom, and stirred vigorously so it smoothed out—maybe a bit burned, but still safe enough. "No reason I can think of."

Chapter Eleven

It was a winter wonderland.

Georgia had been racing about all morning, ensuring every detail was set, but now that the festival was in full swing, she could take a moment to rest against a tall pine. Her eyes wandered the familiar sight once more, looking for anything amiss—anywhere she was needed. Visitors milled about, more pulling in off the grated road and into the parking area.

A large tent with heating lamps covered Malcolm's lawn beside the creek, a host to twenty booths with everything from crafts for the kids, including a gingerbread house decorating contest, to last-minute shopping opportunities. "Holly Jolly Christmas" played through speakers Nate and Malcolm had hooked up in the corners of the tent. Georgia had taken their suggestions and pulled back on her plans for a Battle of the Bands, creating a simple Christmas playlist instead.

Lines of Pineberry residents and visitors alike stood outside the three food trucks, which had served hot beverages, sweet treats, and delicious meals all morning and into the early afternoon. As predicted, the sun had come out, warming things up so that the water in the creek sparkled and the mountainside just beyond glowed with warmth and promise. What remained of the snow added to the holiday ambiance.

Laughter rang out from the inflatable North Pole–themed bounce house, where children called to their parents from inside the netted doors. And speaking of Santa's workshop, Taylor had texted her not thirty minutes ago that pictures with Santa's reindeer were going smoothly in the barn. The photo she'd sent had shown at least twenty kids waiting for their turn with the adorable baby goats.

Things were going as well as could be expected, and ticket sales so far were on track to generate more than enough to meet Nate's goal.

So why did her body slump? Why did her heart catch whenever she thought of what came after this—her return to New York? Not even the enticement of her new position seemed to help her mood.

The position that Nate had congratulated her on last night, but hadn't told her not to take...even when she'd given him the perfect opportunity to tell her she had a reason to stay.

"No reason I can think of."

"There you are." Her grandmother's voice interrupted the memory as Mimi appeared at Georgia's side, Elizabeth in tow. She walked with only a slight limp now, something her physical therapist was confident she'd overcome soon. It was so good to see her looking so vibrant and fresh—her cheeks had much more color than when Georgia had arrived three weeks ago, and her eyes more sparkle.

"Here I am." Georgia leaned in for a quick peck on Mimi's cheek. "Sorry I snuck off before you emerged this morning. Needed to get up here super early." She turned to Elizabeth and smiled. "Are you both having a good time?"

"Oh, it's simply marvelous, Georgia." Elizabeth patted her hand. "You've taken our dinky little festival of years past and raised the bar. I don't know how we will ever top this."

"We're both very proud of you." Mimi wasn't given to

crying, but even she had shimmering eyes. "Thank you for sticking this out and helping our town like this. You did much more than I ever could."

"Thank you for giving me a project while I was in town. It kept me from going stir-crazy."

"It's too bad you won't be here to plan next year's festival," Elizabeth said. "But I've heard congratulations are in order. When do you head back to New York for your new job?"

"Thank you. I'm going home a week from today, so I can—"

"You're leaving?" The small voice behind Georgia wrenched her heart in two.

She turned to find Cassie there, holding Nate's hand. Behind him stood his mom, Linda, stoic as always. Her eyes seemed to watch Georgia, just waiting for her to make a mistake. As for Nate, his eyes were filled with apology, and Cassie's welled with tears.

Oh no. This was not how she'd wanted to tell Cassie of her impending departure. "Hey, Cass. Come here." Georgia held out her hand, but Cassie wouldn't take it—just stayed rooted beside Nate. Okay, then. Georgia retracted her hand and inhaled a deep breath. "You know I live in New York, right? Well, I got a new job and I have to go home soon. But I'll still be here for Christmas, and if it's okay with your dad, we can hang out some more. I can show you how to make Mimi's cookies." She glanced at Mimi, who nodded, her gaze filled with empathy. Or pity, perhaps. Then she refocused on Cassie. "How does that sound?"

"I thought..." Cassie's bottom lip trembled. "I thought you might want to stay with us."

"Oh, Cass." Georgia's own eyes burned and blurred. "I..."

One eyebrow arched, Linda stepped forward and placed a protective hand on Cassie's shoulder. "Georgia has to go back where she belongs, Cassie."

Sucking in a breath, Georgia slumped back against the tree trunk—and Cassie took off sprinting toward the barn.

"Cassie!" Nate huffed out a breath and turned to Linda. "Mom…"

"What? Did I say anything that wasn't true?"

"No, it's just…sorry, I need to go see if she's okay." Shaking his head, Nate strode off in the direction Cassie had run.

Linda turned a self-satisfied smirk toward Georgia, Mimi, and Elizabeth. "Excuse me, ladies." Then she sauntered off toward the tent in her pressed slacks and shoes that were far too fancy to be seen on a farm.

"That woman…" Elizabeth ground out. "Excuse *me* while I go give her a piece of my mind." Then she followed Linda, her head held high and her shoulders erect.

Georgia watched her go, her insides numb. *"Georgia has to go back where she belongs."* The words echoed in her brain. And Nate's response…

"Are you all right, Georgia-girl?" Mimi's gentle murmur brought Georgia back to the moment, and all of her senses crashed back around her at once—the smell of cooked taco meat, the strands of "Sleigh Ride" lilting through the air, the breeze rustling the leaves in the pine above her, sunlight reflecting off the melting snow at her feet.

"What?" Crossing her arms over her chest, she blinked at her grandma.

"Aw, dear. Come with me."

She allowed Mimi to lead her under the large tent, past a group of volunteers helping with the gift wrapping station, over to an empty picnic table Malcolm had donated for the event. The heated space warmed Georgia's chilled bones.

"I'll be right back." Hobbling toward the nearest food truck, Mimi knocked on the door. In moments, it swung open and she was speaking with the owner, pointing at Georgia. What was she up to?

But the answer became clear when minutes later, Mimi came back with a dozen donuts decorated in a Christmas plaid pattern. When Mimi sat across from her, she slid the plate toward Georgia, whose stomach rumbled at the sight and smell of the pastries.

She picked one up. "I probably shouldn't eat this, but I haven't had anything all morning. Been too busy." Taking a bite, she let the sugary taste rush her taste buds. The donut melted in her mouth. "Okay, I needed that."

"Sweets always did make you happy."

"They used to—but this is the first donut I've had in years." She finished it off, too quickly, and reached for a napkin from the metal dispenser in the middle of the wooden table. "Thank you. I should probably get back to checking on things." She started to rise.

"Sit down, young lady." Mimi's voice teased and she winked at her. "Things are running smoothly for now, and I've got something to say."

"Yes, ma'am," Georgia mumbled. "But if it's about what happened earlier, I'm fine. I wish Cassie hadn't found out that way, but she was bound to be upset."

"Because you've grown close."

"Yes." There was no denying the fact.

"And because she sees what the rest of us do—that you and her father have grown close. Perhaps closer than you'd like to admit."

"Mimi, I..." Georgia shook her head. "I won't deny that things between me and Nate are complicated. But we find ourselves at an impasse, with the same exact issues we had years ago."

"My dear, you are not the same people you were back

then. And whatever Linda Griggs says, you *do* belong here. You always have." She reached across the table and gripped Georgia's hand in hers. "I have watched you these last few weeks finding your way. You arrived frosty and unsure, and you have melted before my eyes into someone who is comfortable in her own skin. You know who you are, and you don't need anyone else's approval, because who you are is lovely. Who you are is enough."

"Then why didn't he fight for me?" The question burst from Georgia's lips, surprising her with its clarity. "Maybe I *have* felt different the last few weeks. Maybe I have melted, as you say, and maybe being away from the rigid and unforgiving life I built for myself in New York has been good for me. But the fact still remains, Mimi—Nate Griggs doesn't want me. Not truly. When push comes to shove, he will always choose everything else over me. Now, Cassie, I understand. She's his daughter. He *should* prioritize her needs. But to not even stand up to his mom just now…" She swiped at her eyes. "Nobody my whole life has ever chosen me, and I'm tired of it."

"Excuse me," Mimi said. "What am I? Chopped liver?"

"Of course not. You chose to keep me when you could have sent me away, but you didn't choose me in the way I'm talking about. I was thrust on you, and you did what any decent grandmother would have. But I came in and upended your life—"

"My dear, I always wanted you." Mimi's eyes blazed with something strong—passion, perhaps, a conviction in what she was saying. "In fact, when I saw the kind of life she'd chosen, I begged Brooke more than once to send you to live with me, but she refused to give you up. So don't you dare say no one has ever chosen you."

"I... I didn't know." How foolish she'd been. "I just assumed that I was a burden to you."

"A burden? Goodness, child. You were God's greatest gift to me in a difficult time, when I'd lost everything else. You gave me something worth living for."

Georgia's chin trembled. "Mimi... I'm sorry."

"Don't be sorry. *I'm* sorry that I never told you this before." Mimi grabbed a napkin and leaned forward to wipe Georgia's tears from under her eyes. "And I'd be remiss if I didn't remind you of something else. Even before I came along, even before Nate failed to choose you, as you say—someone else chose you. God sent His son to die for you even before you were born. And if you'd been the only person to ever exist, He would still have chosen pain and suffering so that you could live."

Peace flooded Georgia at the thought—that Someone had chosen her, had fought for her. And she hadn't had to perform at the top of the pack or prove that she was good enough to gain His favor.

All she'd had to do was just *be*.

"Oh, Mimi." She grasped her grandma's hand that cradled Georgia's face. "I've been so worried about measuring up. So worried about what others think. But all along, His opinion mattered most."

"That's right. And He says you are loved, redeemed, and worth dying for." Mimi motioned around them, at the celebration, the trappings of the holiday. "You've spent the last few weeks planning this festival to celebrate Christmas, and it's a wonderful festival. But don't miss the true point of it all—it's staring you right in the face."

Of course it was. "It's about love, isn't it?"

"Yes, dear. Love is the whole point—of the holiday, and life."

* * *

Of course Cassie would be among the goats.

Er—reindeer.

Nate leaned on the gate to the enclosure where Malcolm's goats milled inside the barn at one end. At the other, the North Pole had been created with a large chair, stacked presents, twinkly lights, and Santa himself—aka Pastor Jim—along with Mary (Mrs. Claus) and Caroline dressed as an elf with a goat on a leash. She occasionally traded out the goat for a new one. Nate had been here long enough to see her do it twice.

Meanwhile, he'd seen children of all ages come through to pet the goats. Now one toddler in a puffy pink coat trotted after a goat who clearly didn't want to be touched. A set of boys raced each other around a haystack until Malcolm—who had been quietly propped back against the wall, arms crossed, hat low—plucked them both up by their torsos and plopped them on the other side of the gate beside their scolding mother.

And then there was Cassie, sitting with her back against the gate on the opposite side, clinging to a baby goat who was somehow content to stay in her arms. It broke his heart to see her there, alternately crying and whispering to the goat. He'd tried to talk with her about Georgia's leaving when he'd found her here a half hour ago, but she'd only wanted to snuggle goats.

So, he'd given her space.

But as the minutes ticked by, he couldn't help but blame himself.

"With how well this festival is going, I'd think you'd be jumping for joy, not standing here looking so forlorn."

The rumbling voice at his elbow made Nate turn. Jim had removed his hat, fake beard, and Santa coat and stood there eating a sandwich wrapped in wax paper. At Nate's raised eyebrow, Jim shrugged. "Mrs. Claus is rather bossy and declared it my fifteen-minute break time." He rubbed his padded gut. "My stomach agreed with her."

"Even Santa's gotta eat. Thanks for filling in at the last minute, by the way. When our hired man called in this morning with the stomach flu, Georgia immediately knew you were the man for the job."

"She's got good instincts, that one. I'm enjoying it." Jim took a bite of his sandwich—which smelled like roast beef—and turned toward Cassie. A moment later, he said, "What's wrong with our girl?"

"She's sad because she found out Georgia's leaving next week."

"Ah."

Nate scrubbed a hand over his jaw, roughened with stubble he hadn't had time to shave. "This is my fault, Jim. I should have protected her from this."

"How so?"

"I knew from the beginning that Georgia would leave." He'd known she was destined for better things. She always had been—it was why he hadn't been able to refute his mother's statement that Georgia didn't belong here. While he might wish it so, he couldn't hold her back.

Wouldn't.

"And yet, I let her into our lives. Let her befriend Cassie. And now my only daughter, who lost her mom not two years ago, has been devastated again."

"Kids are much more resilient than we give them credit for."

"She's only seven. How much heartache can one girl take?"

Jim hummed beside him. "Nate, your job isn't to protect her from all heartache."

"I'm her father. If it's not my job, then whose is it? I should have kept Georgia at arm's length. It was selfish of me to..." Nate shook his head. "I should have been thinking of Cassie first."

"From where I'm standing, you did nothing wrong, son. In fact, you're one of the best fathers I've ever met—and I know my fair share."

He turned his gaze sharply on Jim, narrowed his eyes. "How can you possibly say that? Didn't you just hear how I failed her?"

"Nate, it's not your job to protect her from every bad thing that could ever happen. Do you think you're God?"

The question stunned him. "Of course not. But if protecting her isn't my job, then what is?"

"To show her how to lean on God when bad things happen. Because they will." Jim rewrapped the rest of his sandwich and set it on the flat fence post. A herd of baby goats came closer, sniffing the air, and Jim chuckled. "Animals. They're creatures of habit, of instinct, and while we are of course different in that God made us in His image, a lot of times we are just like them, aren't we?"

"How so?"

"Our instinct is to try to run from pain, to do whatever we must to not feel or experience it. But pain is part of life. We must face it—but we don't have to face it alone. You were never meant to bear the burden of your pain alone, and you were never meant to parent Cassie all alone. God wants to be your safe place, Nate. He wants to bear your pain with you. For you."

His hands fisted the top of the fence. "I don't know how to let Him do that."

"Stop running away from the pain...away from Him. And stop thinking you have to be likable and compliant in order to be respected and loved. That has never been the case for God. Don't box him in, Nate. He can handle your questions, your doubts, your anger. Don't put conditions on His love for you. He will blow your assumptions out of the water every time."

"I don't deserve it." Nate's breath shuddered, and he pressed the ridge of his nose between his thumb and forefinger. "I've done things I'm not proud of, Jim. Stephanie and I…"

"None of us deserve grace, and God knows that, but He gives it anyway. And my Stephanie wasn't perfect either." Jim's smile was kindness itself. "But she knew something we all knew—you're a good man, Nate Griggs. You love people, especially that little girl in there."

A tear trickled down Nate's cheek and he pressed against his eyelids. "Thank you, Jim."

"I'm not saying it to be nice. I'm speaking the truth. And the truth is, you can't be all things to her, Nate. You can't save and protect her from everything. You can only point her to Jesus, because more than anything, she needs a Savior."

"You're right. She does." He blew out a breath. "I just don't want to screw this up. It's too important."

"Oh, you'll mess up plenty. All of us mere mortals do." Jim laughed, then sobered as he clapped a hand on Nate's shoulder. "But that's what grace is for." Someone called for him, and he looked over his shoulder. "The missus is summoning me again. I've got children waiting. But if you need me, I'm here, all right?"

"I'm blessed to have you in my life, Jim. Thank you."

His father-in-law pulled Nate into a bear hug and hurried back to his workshop.

Meanwhile, Nate turned to find Cassie in the same lonely place, hugging the same goat, the same mournful expression on her face. He still felt helpless—but now he knew where to turn for help. "Lord…give me the words." Then he swung through the gate and approached his daughter, plopping onto the ground beside her.

She glanced up, big eyes filled with tears. "Why do people we love always gotta leave, Daddy?"

"Aw, baby." He slung his arm around her and pulled her into his lap. She snuggled against his chest. "People might leave us, but you know who never will?"

She pulled back and scrunched up her nose. "Who?"

"God." And as they sat there surrounded by smelly goats who tried to eat Nate's pants and made Cassie giggle, he told her all about the One who would always be there—in the good times and bad—no matter what.

Chapter Twelve

Nate's new resolve to ask God to help bear his pain meant the Big Guy was working overtime as of late...because Georgia was never far from his mind.

He missed her, and she hadn't even left town yet. But in the two days since the festival, he also hadn't seen her once—a small taste of the absence he would soon be experiencing if he didn't do something about it.

And, oh, how he wanted to do something about it. But before he could promise her anything, or make a leap of faith, he had to free himself from the expectations of others.

Tonight was the night when he would test Jim's theory about whether he'd continue to be loved and respected if he didn't do what others requested—nay, demanded—of him. He'd told his parents when he'd arrived at Dad's retirement dinner that he needed to speak with them, but Mom had been rushing around the kitchen and Dad promised they'd sit down later to talk.

Now, after a half hour, Nate took a sip from his water goblet and looked around his parents' table where his whole family minus his older sister, Eleanor—who was teaching English overseas—had gathered. His sister Aimee had just arrived from Los Angeles, where she worked long hours as a first-year attorney. Christian and his mother, Nancy, sat to the right of Dad, who was at the head of the table, and Mom and Cassie were across from them.

They'd all been talking and laughing over Mom's elegant meal of roast and potatoes, but as good as it smelled, Nate hadn't tasted a bite he'd shoveled in. Nobody had seemed to notice his quiet except for Mom, who gave him a concerned look.

Could she read his mind? Know what he wanted to talk to them about? But how could she? He'd given no indication of it...ever.

It would likely come as a shock to them, but it had to be done.

He had to tell them he didn't want to be CEO if he was going to be free to pursue the things that truly made him happy.

Mom tapped her flute of cider with a spoon and stood, adjusting her strand of pearls with one hand while holding her drink aloft with the other. "Thank you all for coming to this monumental celebration. Steve and I are so grateful to call you each family, and though I offered to throw him a huge retirement bash, he insisted that all he needed was a quiet dinner at home with his family."

Everyone chuckled and aahed, and Dad waved them all off. "Now, now, there's no need for all the fuss."

"Speech, speech, speech," Christian called, and soon Cassie and Aimee had joined in the fun.

Rolling his eyes good-naturedly, Dad finally gave in. "Not much to say, except that I've had a good career. I'm grateful for it, and I'll miss parts of it, but—" he turned his gaze to Nate and lifted his flute toward him "—I know the company will be in good hands."

Nate swallowed, his throat dry. He felt all the eyes on him, Christian's boring into him the hardest of all. This wasn't the right time to contradict him, but he also couldn't very well agree with Dad. So he said nothing.

But Mom wouldn't let it go. "Don't be shy, Nathaniel. Dazzle us all with your CEO speech-giving skills."

The table chuckled, and Cassie's smile flashed big and wide at him. She was looking up to him, expectant, no idea that he was struggling.

And he wanted to show her that was okay too.

"About that." Nate rubbed his finger down his flute, leaving a fingerprint trail in the condensation. "Dad, I don't..." His gaze flicked toward Christian, who nodded his encouragement. Whew. *Lord, give me strength.* "I'm actually thinking about maybe taking another job."

Silence fell. Aimee blinked at him like he had two heads. Christian sat back in his seat, arms folded over his chest, which was puffed out like a proud papa bear. Dad looked at him thoughtfully. And Mom...well, she was giving him a very "Mom" look.

"What do you mean, another job?" she said. "This job has been intended for you since you were born. Sure, you took a few years off from construction to be mayor—which we are very proud of—but now it's time to get back to the plan."

"But it isn't my plan, Mom. It's yours. It's always been yours. And I want something different."

"This is because of that girl, isn't it?" Mom hissed.

Cassie's head darted to the right, where Mom sat, then back to Nate. "What girl, Daddy?"

Aunt Nancy pushed herself up—as quickly as she could, given her multiple sclerosis—setting her napkin onto her mostly cleaned plate. "Cassie, why don't we go watch some *Grinch*? I heard it's your favorite."

Cassie clapped. "Ooh, yay!" She leaped up.

"Christian, Aimee?" Aunt Nancy said.

The two reluctantly followed her out, but not before Christian pumped his fist at Nate and mouthed, "You've got this, bro."

Once it was just Nate and his parents, he got up and moved to their side of the table. "I didn't mean to spring that on you. I'm sorry for that." He pushed Christian's plate out of the way and set his elbows on the table.

Mom glared at the place his arms met the wood, but he did not move them.

"And to answer your question, Mom, no—this is not because of Georgia, though she has inspired me in a lot of ways."

"I knew it. I knew she wasn't good for you."

"Are you hearing me, Mom? She inspires me. She's too good for me, really, and yet…"

"You love her." Dad finally said something—and it was succinct, to the point. Simple.

And true.

"I do."

"No, you don't." Mom flicked her napkin in the air. "You only think you do because you're missing Stephanie. Now *there* was good wife material. Such a shame God took her so young."

Nate rubbed his temples. "It is a shame, and yes, Stephanie was a great wife. But that has nothing to do with Georgia, who I personally think would make an amazing wife too. And a great mother for Cassie." He cleared his throat. "But that's not what this is about. This is about me, clearing the decks for what I want in life. And that means saying no to your job offer, Dad. I'm sorry. I know this leaves you in the lurch, though I believe Christian would make an even better CEO than me."

"Something to consider." Dad scratched his chin. "Do you mind me asking what it is you *do* want?"

"He doesn't know what he wants." Mom got up and began pacing behind her chair. "She has him all confused."

"Mom, I'm right here."

Mom huffed. "I know, Nathaniel. But you're not thinking straight. We're your parents. It's our job—"

"Linda, he's a grown man."

Her mouth flopped open and she halted. "Of course he is. But he's still my child."

Dad opened his mouth to speak, but Nate beat him to it. It was finally time to stand up for what he wanted. "And I love you, Mom, but Dad's right. I'm grown. You guys raised me to love people and God, and I'm doing my best here. I'd like to think you're proud of that." He cocked his head. "But even if you're not, I still have to make the best decisions I can make—set the best example for Cassie as I can. And I want her to someday follow her passions and talents. So I have to do that too."

"But…" Mom sputtered. "What's wrong with taking over as CEO of Griggs Construction? It's a perfectly respectable life."

"There's nothing wrong with it. But it's not me. I hate the parts of my job that deal with the business-y side of things. I love people…kids especially. And while some parts of being mayor have been rewarding and have taught me how to work with a variety of different personality types, I want to do something with my life that I find personally meaningful."

"And what's that?" Dad asked, his exterior as calm as his voice.

"I want to apply to be director of the community center." He waited, and his pause was met with expectant silence, as if urging him to keep going. "But I also want to pursue a relationship with Georgia. And I'm not sure what that looks like, but I'm ready to fight for her like I didn't do thirteen years ago."

"Nathaniel." Mom sighed, closing her eyes momentarily like she was praying for patience. "Think about what you're saying. That girl could have you moving across the country, and that would hardly make you happy! Cassie would be miserable. And us, well—"

"I think it's a wonderful thing."

Dad's words surprised both Nate and his mom, if the way her lips flopped open were any indication.

"You do?" Nate asked.

"Marrying your mother has been the greatest joy of my life." He reached back and took Mom's hand in his. The stunned expression on her face almost made Nate chuckle. But then, her expression melted. Her eyes softened, and he could see in her the girl she maybe had once been. A woman who hadn't dealt with the hard knocks of life, who hadn't become a parent bent on controlling her children.

In fact, maybe Mom had struggled the way Nate had—wanting to protect him from hurt by mapping out his life for him.

But even if he understood her, that didn't mean he had to give in to her. "I want what you guys have. And I think Georgia could make me happy. So I'm going to do something about it—what that means, I'm not sure. We will figure it out together. If she wants me to." He straightened in his seat. "And I know I don't need your blessing, but I'd like it all the same."

"We want you to be happy," Dad said. "So of course we give you our blessing, son. Don't we, Linda?" He patted his wife's hand.

She studied Nate, her lips pursed. "It's all I've ever

wanted. For you to be happy. But are you sure Georgia Carrington is the way to make that happen?"

"All I know is that I'll regret it forever if I don't see for sure. And I'm sorry if that puts us at odds, Mom. That's not what I want. But I'm willing to risk it if it means a chance to fight for the woman I love."

"You Griggs men are all alike." She sighed. "Sentimental old fools." But her arms wound around Dad's shoulders, and she set her chin on top of his head.

"I'll take that as a compliment." Dad winked at Nate. "Now...how are you planning to fight for that woman of yours?"

"I honestly haven't a clue. You got any brilliant ideas?"

If love was the point of life, then Georgia hadn't really been living. Not really.

She'd spent the last thirteen years isolated, given over to the pursuit of something that—in the end—had left her alone, hollow, filled with anxiety over the idea that she'd never be enough.

But no more.

No matter what came next, Georgia was not going to live her life in isolation anymore. Which was why she'd sent the email early this Christmas Eve morning.

The one that still freaked her out if she thought about it too much.

She climbed from her SUV in front of the Walker B&B and, proposal in hand, marched it up the front steps. Guests milled about the front room, some enjoying a delicious-smelling brunch at the long table in the dining area, others gathered in front of the large tree in the corner exchanging gifts.

Eloise's Christmas tree earrings dangled as she looked up and smiled. "Merry Christmas Eve, Ms. Carrington."

"Merry Christmas to you too." She placed the proposal on the desk and slid it toward Wayne's granddaughter. "Can you please make sure your grandfather gets this?"

"He's here if you'd like to give it to him yourself."

"I'm actually late for something, but please let him know I'll be in town a little longer than I thought. So if he has questions, he can call and I'll happily come in. And please make sure he reads the résumé I included, along with the cover letter." She winked at the younger woman.

"You've got it." Eloise took the proposal and stood. "I'll run it to him now. Wish I could get him to take today of all days off, but the man is a workaholic."

"You're working too, I see."

Eloise shrugged. "Someone has to make sure the guests have what they need."

"And they're blessed it's you." With a final wave, Georgia took off out the door and popped in her vehicle, then drove straight to Caroline's shop. The sign was flipped to Closed in front of Pineberry Treasures, but Georgia headed around to the side, where a staircase led to the second story.

Caroline answered Georgia's knock and pulled her inside the small apartment. "Come in, come in," she said with a hug. The place could only be four hundred square feet in total—with its galley kitchen, small living room boasting a simple couch and TV stand, and short hallway leading to Caroline's bedroom, one small guest room, and single bathroom—but it was warm and cozy and so very Caroline with its cheery yellow paint and a large painting of a beach somewhere hanging on the wall behind the couch. In her kitchen, an assortment of colorful mugs hung from hooks under her white cabinets, and a four-person table had been shoved into the corner. "Taylor's already here."

"Hey, there!" Taylor called as she came out of the bathroom, a tie-dyed long-sleeve sweater brightening her face, which looked a bit pale and drawn. She grabbed Georgia into a hug and pointed to the kitchen counter. "I brought coffee and donuts to our little pre-Christmas brunch."

Laughing, Georgia unwound her scarf. "Living here is going to make me fat."

Her friends exchanged glances, then fixed their eyes back on Georgia. "Living here?" Caroline asked.

Georgia removed her purse and tossed it onto the couch. "Oh, did I forget to tell you? I sent in my resignation letter today."

"What?" Caroline jumped up and down, then threw another hug Georgia's way. "This is the best news ever."

"It's really great," Taylor said, her expression cautious. "What are you planning to do?"

"I don't have anything lined up for sure." Georgia strode to the kitchen, threw open the box of donuts, and snagged one. "But I spent the last three days working on the joint community center proposal for Wayne, and when I turned it in, I may have included a cover letter and my own résumé, expressing interest in the parks and rec director position I spent hours creating to fit my specific skill set." She made a face.

"Ooh, I love that." Caroline hip bumped her out of the way and snagged a chocolate long John. "You're a shoo-in for sure—even though I have no idea what a parks and rec director does." She popped a piece of her donut into her mouth, chewed, smiled. "So what made you decide to stay? Does it have anything to do with someone whose name rhymes with date?"

Taylor snickered. "Is that the best you can do?" She leaned against the countertop. "But seriously, *does* it have to do with him?"

Georgia chewed her lip, and placed her donut on a paper towel, licking caramelized sugar from her fingertips. "It has to do with me. I've been hiding away, trying to be somebody important. But I realized I already was somebody important, and I wasn't truly happy with my job. It was something I thought I *had* to do…but really, the long hours and all the competition were wearing me out so much, distracting me from finding love. From visiting Mimi. From spending time with my best friends in the world—"

"And by that, you mean us, right?"

"She definitely means us." Caroline nodded.

"I definitely do."

"What did Nate say when you told him?" Taylor asked.

"Um. Well."

"You *have* told him, right?" Caroline gasped when Georgia winced.

"Not exactly." She hurried on. "I had to be sure I was doing this for me, that I had the guts to resign before I even attempted to speak with him about it. But we're meeting at our spot soon—he texted me last night and asked if we could talk. And we haven't spoken since the festival, so I'm assuming he wants to clear the air, to make sure we're still friends."

"I'm *sure* that's all he wants to say." Taylor rolled her eyes. "Girl, the way he looks at you…that man does *not* want to just be your friend."

Georgia's hand twitched at her side. "I hope you're right. But even if not, I'm determined to be okay."

"And you will." Caroline reached for her hand, then for Taylor's. "We all are going to be okay, no matter what troubles we face. Because we have God, and we have each other. That's all we need."

Georgia opened her mouth to agree, but Taylor's eyes grew misty.

"Tay? You all right?" she asked.

"Who, me? Yeah. Of course." Her friend's voice broke. "I just needed to hear that things will be okay."

"Why?" Georgia grasped Taylor's other hand. "What's going on with you?"

"Um." Taylor, always so strong and independent, slumped. "The reason I moved back is..." She shut her eyes. "I'm pregnant."

Oh, wow. "Tay...that's a lot."

"I'm due in early July. The father and I...we aren't together." She didn't offer anything more, and now wasn't the time to ask for details. "I'm doing this alone."

But that...now *that* statement Georgia couldn't abide. "You absolutely are not. You've got Malcolm. And we're here."

"Yeah," Caroline said, her chin jutted, her eyes fierce. "This baby's gonna have two of the best aunties ever...and maybe he or she will even get grouchy Uncle Malcolm to crack a smile."

"That'd be the day." Taylor laughed through her tears. Then she sobered. "Thank you both. I've been afraid to tell you, but I can't avoid the truth—or the consequences of my actions—any longer. I know God's forgiven me, and I just have to keep moving forward the best way I know how. I won't fail this child."

They hugged and sat down on the couch snuggled close, eating donuts, drinking coffee, and reminiscing about the good old days of high school, and the hour frittered by quickly. When Georgia got up to leave, she felt the zing of the coffee to her toes.

Or maybe that was just the anticipation of seeing Nate again.

"I say you walk right up to the man and plant one on him," Taylor said.

Caroline laughed. "Can I be a fly on the tunnel wall?"

"Just because we kissed one time and he said he'd always care for me doesn't mean he wants more than that. He's got Cassie to consider. Plus I don't want a man who won't fight for me. Or who only wants me if it's convenient." Georgia threw her scarf on and played with the fringed ends. "And we all know his mom still doesn't approve of me."

"You're not in high school anymore." Taylor rubbed her stomach, sighing. "None of us is."

"I think what Taylor's trying to say is...we've all lived enough to know that life is short." Caroline offered a sad smile. "And living for others' approval instead of God's will never bring us true joy."

"Yes, exactly that." Taylor nodded, eyes sparking. "I'm very wise."

They all laughed, and after a round of hugs, Georgia was headed out the door. She had to keep her foot soft on the gas when all she wanted to do was gun it all the way to the path that would lead her to Nate.

To their bridge.

Once there, though, she sat in the vehicle for a while, staring at the azure sky, at the landmark in the distance. A place of so much pain, yes, but also love. A place where they'd started off as children without a clue as to who they were...and had now become adults with a solid assurance of Whose they were and where they belonged.

Climbing from the car, Georgia started down the path that would bring her to the man she loved, her heart rate increasing with every step. The snow along the trail was mostly melted, and the sun shone through a few clouds—perhaps a promise, that no matter what darkness there may be, Light would always break through.

Finally, she reached the bridge and headed into the tunnel, where—atop their rock—Nate stood, hands in his jeans pockets.

Waiting for her.

They didn't say a word as she climbed over boulders to be with him, and when she finally reached him, huffing a bit from the ascent, they faced each other, staring. He regarded her in a tender way, his eyes welcoming her without words.

"Hi," he said at last.

"Hi."

"Thanks for coming." He shifted from one foot to the other. "I didn't know if you would."

"Of course I came." Georgia cocked her head, studied him. "We're friends, after all."

"Right." He coughed. "Friends."

Her shoulders sank at his confirmation. But whether Nate fought for their relationship or not, she was going to be okay—because she had a warrior King who would always pursue her relentlessly.

Still, she'd hoped... "So what did you want to talk about?"

Nate pulled his ungloved hand from his pocket and extended it toward her, a silent asking for her to take it. Without looking away, she removed her own glove and tucked her hand in his, palm against palm. He focused on the sight for a few long moments before speaking.

"Georgia—Peach—these past few weeks have been..." His deep inhalation rattled her nerves, as did the way his thumb stroked the top of her knuckles. "They've been eye-opening. I'd been going through life, content to let others decide what my life would look like because I was desperately afraid to lose anyone else I cared about. And then you came breaking back in—"

"I told you… I had a key." She smiled as he chuckled, and his laugh went straight to her heart.

"I didn't expect you, Georgia. And then, when you were here, I told myself you'd changed. That you were too big-city for us. That you'd always thought you were better than us, and that's why you left. But I was wrong."

Oh, Nate. "I'm sorry I ever made you feel that way."

"And I'm sorry you felt you had to go away to prove something. That you felt like you didn't belong here. But, Peach, you do. In fact—" he stepped closer and held their bound hands to his chest, his gaze piercing her with its steadiness "—you belong right here. With me. You always have. I love you, Georgia Carrington, and I will do whatever it takes to make this work between us. I know you're leaving, but I have faith in this, and in God who brought us together, that we can find a way. And I won't stop fighting to figure that out. That is…if you love me too."

"Love you?" Georgia's eyes filled with tears. "Of course I love you. How could I not? But what about your parents? They won't like this."

"My dad loves this, and my mom is coming around."

Wait. "You told them you loved me?"

"Monday night I told them that two things would make me happy—to *not* be CEO of Griggs Construction, and to pursue a relationship with you."

"What?" Her jaw dropped. "You really did that?"

"Don't sound so surprised." His smile turned more sober. "And I know we aren't technically even dating yet, but I see a future with you and want you to know how serious I am. How much I want to build a life with you. To show you each and every day that you belong, that you were made for my arms."

"Nate." Laugh-crying with joy, she cupped his cheeks with her hands. "That's beautiful."

"You're beautiful, and you make my life beautiful. Cassie and I would be more than blessed to have you in our lives on a permanent basis. But we can go slowly, in your timing. Whatever you need. I don't want to scare you away, but I just…you're it for me, Peach. I'm all in."

"You won't scare me. I'm all in too." Going up on her tiptoes, she pressed a kiss to his mouth, and he met it with equal enthusiasm. For several long moments, they made new memories here—ones she'd never forget.

Finally, they pulled back, and Nate placed his forehead against hers. "So I guess we need to think about how this is going to work between us. I was looking at job opportunities in New York, and—"

"You were?"

"Of course. I know how much that promotion means to you, and so Cassie and I will need to come to you. And while I'm sure that will be hard, it'll also be an adventure. An adventure we undertake together."

This man. He would really sacrifice so much for her?

How amazing to know he was willing—but she was grateful to know he didn't have to. "The thing about an adventure," she said, "is that we can have one right here."

His brow furrowed. "What do you mean?"

"I mean…" Georgia bit the inside of her cheek and looked away momentarily. "I only thought I wanted the promotion, but my motives were all wrong. When I stopped and considered what really made me happy, where I felt most loved and valued, it's right here in Pineberry with Mimi, Taylor, Caroline…with you and Cassie. So I quit my job."

"You…quit?"

"I quit." She grinned. "And I also kind of unofficially applied for a position working for the new mayor of Pineberry."

His arm looped around her waist and he pulled her to his chest. "You are full of surprises. But are you sure?"

"I'm sure that if I leave you again, I will regret it forever." She rubbed her thumb along a button on his shirt. "But it's not just you. While I do think we could be happy anywhere, I'm seeing Pineberry differently than I did. It's the first real home I ever had where I felt safe. The first place that welcomed me in, a few residents notwithstanding. And it's in Pineberry that I can hear myself think, that I can have that work-life balance I've heard so many rumors about." She smiled. "And most importantly, it's here where I fell in love with you, not just once, but twice, Mr. Mayor."

"Here is a pretty good place, then." He nuzzled her nose and kissed the tip of it. "But you know…as of next week, I won't be the mayor. You can't go calling me that anymore."

"True. I'll have to think of something else, I guess." She snagged the lapels of his jacket and brought him closer. "*Boyfriend* should do quite nicely." Georgia winked. "For now."

"I like the way you think. Merry Christmas, Georgia."

"Merry Christmas, Nate."

And as he kissed her softly, no more doubts between them, it was very merry indeed.

Epilogue

One year later

The Pineberry Community Center—with its high ceilings, multiple rooms, and extensive outdoor space—made the perfect venue for the annual Christmas festival, which was in full swing.

Georgia's team of volunteers had strung lights everywhere. A pair of twenty-foot decorated trees flanked the edges of the entrance. Booths lined the basketball court and a stage at one end hosted the next round of singers for Battle of the Holiday Bands. A sweet quartet of men in flashing reindeer ties and Santa hats currently serenaded the whole center with "White Christmas."

Gripping her clipboard, Georgia roamed the activity stations in the middle of the room, making sure all was in order. Happy squeals rose from children doing the Christmas cookie walk—a substitute cakewalk—and from here she could spy the blow-up bounce house shaped like a gingerbread house just out the back doors.

"Georgia!"

She turned to find Cassie and Mimi sitting at the table where guests could decorate their own ornaments. "Hey, ladies. You having fun?" She walked closer to inspect their projects.

"So much fun." Cassie held up an ornament, her hands covered in red glitter. "Look, I made one for Mommy. It's an angel like the ones she's probably singing with today."

"It's lovely."

"And now I'm gonna make one for Asher."

Over Cassie's head, Mimi smiled and pressed a hand to her chest. "I can't think of anything better than that, can you, Georgia?"

Her heart squeezed. "I can't. We can all hang it up together when we get home, how about that?"

"Okay!"

Someone called for Georgia. "I've gotta go. Have fun, you two." She mouthed a thank-you to Mimi for watching Cassie and turned toward the sound of her name.

Linda approached, hands on both hips. "Georgia Griggs, just what do you think you're doing?"

Georgia's mouth opened to protest, but her mother-in-law only tsked and led her to a chair near the food booths. "You promised you'd take it easy today."

She actually hadn't promised anything, but one didn't argue with Linda Griggs. Still, she had a job to do. "I—"

"Ah, ah, ah." Her mother-in-law pushed another chair up under Georgia's feet and whipped the clipboard right out of her hands. "You will not go into early labor on my watch. That grandson of mine needs six more weeks to bake, and that's what he's going to get."

Many women in Georgia's position might roll their eyes, but the fact that Linda had come around so much after Nate and Georgia's whirlwind courtship and subsequent engagement—they'd only lasted two weeks before deciding that a quick and quiet wedding was exactly what they both wanted—was a testament to God's grace and the power of forgiveness.

So instead, she mumbled, "Yes, ma'am" and smiled at the slight upward self-satisfied curling of Linda's lip and the way she whisked away to boss someone else around.

Georgia reached into her pocket and pulled out her phone, groaning at the effort it took thanks to the very large belly she was sporting. Actually, sitting did feel pretty good, but as parks and rec director, she still had a responsibility to make sure the festival went off without a hitch. She shot off a text to Taylor and Caroline asking them to keep an eye out for Linda and make sure she wasn't on the warpath.

Caroline sent back a thumbs-up, and Taylor a silly GIF of a linebacker tackling a quarterback. She was about to text back that nobody should be tackling anyone when someone tapped a microphone and said, "Is this thing on?"

That voice was the only one who could bring Georgia's body instant calm, and she turned her attention to the man at the front—the man she loved, had always loved.

Nate's gaze, as always, found her in the crowd. He looked so handsome in his dark jeans and green shirt with the sleeves rolled to his elbows. "Thank you for coming out today to support our little town and celebrate the holidays with us. I hope you've all had a fabulous time."

The crowd whooped and cheered.

"For those who don't know me, I'm Nate Griggs, the director of this fabulous community center, which didn't even exist a year ago. Normally it's the mayor of our town who gives these speeches, but Mayor Walker has graciously allowed me the stage today to tell you a little bit more about what the last year has meant to me."

He nodded to Wayne, who sat at a table not too far from Georgia. The mayor tipped his large hat to the crowd and smiled, ever the politician—but, as Georgia had come to know, a good man through and through.

Nate continued. "Thanks to the work of so many—including my wonderful wife, Georgia, who has worked countless hours, and a whole team of volunteers—this center has become a place of refuge not just for the youth and seniors of Pineberry, but for all of us. It's given us a place to gather, a place to play, a place to bond." He cleared his throat, and even from across the room, Georgia could feel the emotion in his words. "A place to heal."

Clapping met Nate's words as he continued to outline what they did here at the center, about the programs they had and the ways they'd been able to reach the community of Pineberry and surrounding areas. "And of course, thank you to each one of you. Without your support here and throughout the year, in the form of time and donations given, we wouldn't have the opportunity to pour into the lives of our residents in all the ways we have. It's been a good year indeed, and I look forward to many, many more. Now, let's get back to celebrating!"

Georgia joined the others in clapping as another band hopped up on stage behind Nate and started a rousing rendition of "Oh, Holy Night." Her husband started moving through the crowd toward her, clapping people on the back as they tried to stop them, but continuing his progress toward her. She struggled to her feet and moved toward the doorway to Nate's office, which once upon a time had been the construction foreman's office.

Leaning back, she waited for him there.

He finally made it to her and leaned against the opposite doorjamb. "I'm shocked to find you standing still."

"Your mother stole my clipboard."

Nate snorted. "Can't say I'm surprised." He crossed his

arms over his chest. "It's all a massive success, Peach. You should be proud."

"I am. And you should be too." She nodded toward the stage. "That was a good speech. Almost like you've had practice talking in front of a crowd."

The edge of his lips hiked upward. "I used to be mayor, you know."

"Oh, yeah. Back when you were important and had the keys to the city."

Nate leaned forward slightly. "The only keys I care about are the ones to your heart."

Now it was her turn to snort. "Did you really just say that?"

"What can I say? I guess marriage and parenthood bring out the cheese in me." He placed a hand on Georgia's stomach, his thumb stroking the rounded edge. "Hear that, little man? You have the cheesiest dad in history."

"Yes, Asher, you certainly do." She feigned an annoyed look at Nate. "Now, if you don't mind…" She started to move away, but he snatched her hand and hauled her back to him.

"Just where do you think you're going?"

"Oh, I don't know. To finish running this festival?"

"You mean the one practically running itself, Wife?"

Ha! "Yes, that one, Husband."

"Fine." His hands slunk around her waist to her lower back. "But not until I get my kiss."

"What kiss?"

He pointed to the top of the doorway, where a little sprig of greenery hung above their heads. "My mistletoe kiss."

She slapped his shoulder. "Did you hang that there?" How had she not noticed it earlier?

"I may have had plans to get you over here at some point today. And then, here you were, drawn toward it all on your own." He tightened his grip around her waist and pulled her as close as possible given the pregnant belly between them. "So. Are you going to kiss me or not, Wife?"

"Hmm." She pretended to think on it, then finally smiled. "I suppose given the choice between kissing you and not kissing you… I will always choose kissing you."

"And that, Mrs. Griggs, will always be the right answer."

And Nate swooped in and claimed her kiss—the one that had always belonged to him.

* * * * *

Dear Reader,

Thanks so much for reading Nate and Georgia's story! It was a true joy bringing them to life on the page (and dear Cassie too!).

I've written several books that take place overseas, and many by the beach, but for this book I wanted to write a little closer to home. Pineberry is actually based on the twin towns of Pine and Strawberry, Arizona, where some of my close family members live.

When considering a location for this book, I couldn't think of anything better than this adorable area known for its lavender honey, awesome hiking trails and outdoor activities, and small-town charm. Many of the places in the book—such as PIEbar and the lavender farm where Malcolm lives—are based loosely on real locales.

Thank you again for reading. I pray you leave this story feeling hope and knowing, above all, that you are loved.

Hugs,
Lindsay

Harlequin® Reader Service

Enjoyed your book?

Try the perfect subscription for Romance readers and get more great books like this delivered right to your door.

See why over 10+ million readers have tried Harlequin Reader Service.

Start with a Free Welcome Collection with free books and a gift—valued over $20.

Choose any series in print or ebook.
See website for details and order today:

TryReaderService.com/subscriptions